We, the Casertas

ALSO BY AURORA VENTURINI

Cousins

We, the Casertas

A Novel

Aurora Venturini

TRANSLATED FROM THE SPANISH BY KIT MAUDE

Soft Skull

New York

First Soft Skull Press edition: 2025

Library of Congress Cataloging-in-Publication Data
Names: Venturini, Aurora, author. | Maude, Kit, translator.
Title: We, the Casertas : a novel / Aurora Venturini ; translated from the Spanish by Kit Maude.
Other titles: Nosotros, los Caserta. English
Description: First Soft Skull Press edition. | New York : Soft Skull, 2025.
Identifiers: LCCN 2024061929 | ISBN 9781593767310 (trade paperback) | ISBN 9781593767327 (ebook)
Subjects: LCGFT: Novels.
Classification: LCC PQ7797.V4214 N6713 2025 | DDC 863/.64—dc23/ eng/20241230
LC record available at https://lccn.loc.gov/2024061929

Cover design by Nicole Caputo
Cover photograph © Sebastián Freire
Book design by Wah-Ming Chang

Soft Skull Press
New York, NY
www.softskull.com

Printed in the United States of America
10 9 8 7 6 5 4 3 2 1

For my Caserta cousins
and Tomasi di Lampedusa

Ore che hai ucciso
Il mio amore,
Si è oscurato il mare,
Mentre il mio cuore
é pieno di dolore.

¡Amore!
FUOCO DI PAGLIA

. . . and I have almost had the impression that what I
have written on these pages, which you will now read,
unknown reader, is only a cento, a figured hymn, an
immense acrostic that says and repeats nothing but
what those fragments have suggested to me, nor do I
know whether, thus far, I have been speaking of them
or they have spoken through my mouth.

UMBERTO ECO

. . . Pictoribus atque poetis
Quidlibet audendi semper fuit
Aequa potestas.

HORACE

We, the Casertas

The Photograph

It was in a doctor's waiting room in La Plata that a vision of Luís's head, a crumbling capital, came back to me, horrifically superimposed between the shoulders of his second wife. I know that I have lost him now and forever, that I shall never again feel his sweet touch, which once belonged to me, because his second marriage must have been a happy union. It is the only reason she would have been able to salvage his head from death, to preserve the features of the only human I ever loved. As part of a normal relationship at least, because I also loved my great-aunt with a passion.

On the long winter nights, I used to hug myself, warmed by fantasies about our loving reunion in the lilac-blue light, the shade of the faithful dead. I now know that he is waiting for her alone, perhaps so she can give him back his head. My mother used to say that married couples who reach old age having maintained a close, harmonious relationship come to seem like siblings. It wasn't true of her, because my mother bore a resemblance to Mr. Roux. But that's another story.

After my confrontation with Luis's widow, even though nothing and nobody can scratch, break, or mutilate me anymore, I've been through it all already, I feel an awful horror. The prospect of being completely, definitively, and horrendously displaced now lies before me: I shall shed rivers of tears into Lake Styx after going through the customary seven circles of Hell and ending up in the garret of the next world. I envy the woman. I envy her widowhood. What I wouldn't give to be Luis's widow. I, who was never anything to anyone.

Repeated slings and arrows have molded me into a simulacrum of my great-aunt, and perhaps the little woman is waiting for me at the threshold of the arcane mystery, beckoning to me so we can cross through together. I limp up to my attic. The repulsive beast I have become searches through an ancient chest of papers and photographs, teachers' and psychologists' reports commissioned by my father to find out just what kind of monster he had sired, to learn whether it was his fault or the effect of some insidious flaw in the maternal line.

I can fit inside, and even get lost in the chest, together with my old woman/dwarf/Proustian soul. After everything I've been through, it's all I've amounted to.

Perhaps unnecessarily, I repeat that I am a woman going through a chest of letters, photographs, reports, cards, and yellowing papers. From out of it pops a little girl in an organdy dress: a photo of me when I was four years old. Along with it leaps Dürer's *Allegory of Melancholy*. It was in a frame once, but I took out it out to store in the chest.

Soon I shall describe the little girl in the organdy dress, but beforehand I shall describe the present state of my soul because I am Albrecht Dürer's Allegory of Melancholy and my surroundings are the same as those of the character.

The attic of my country house contains all the objects of my exile, surrounding me while I lean my pale, feverish head on my left hand. In my right I hold the compasses of futile expectation. Also here are the ladder to nowhere, the cupid on the rusty wheel, the broken bell, the frozen hourglass, the unbalanced scales, and the starving dog. All that are lacking are the symbols Dürer added to the engraving representing hope, the star in the background and the seal of sixteen numbers that add up to thirty-four in every direction, ensuring an eloquent solution to any problem.

The little girl.

She is holding a wicker basket containing paper roses. That

girl is my past self, a gremlin haunting the realm of my future sorrows while I bury my arm up to the elbow in the chests of autumn and the inevitable winter to come.

I had begun my time in Hell four years before the photograph: the day of my birth. An alert girl, a worm in a cocoon she unpicked and reweaved so as to convulse, rise and burst forth, sometimes serene, others obsessive, always precocious.

I look at the photo and I can see my mother on the day she brought me to have it taken.

It was a warm but rainy summer afternoon. The turbulent sky covered the ashen city in metallic gray, acid zinc cloud. We were both sweating, annoying beads of sweat appearing on our foreheads as we sat on the green leather seats of the buggy drawn by a dark horse. I look at the shoes in the photo, which are red with a buckle. Water splashed on them and I tried to dry them with my fine handkerchief but my mother cuffed my head. I see the gold chain with the Alpine cameo medallion, which got tangled up in my silver thread purse. I tugged on it and my mother hit me again.

I can feel the rough green leather of the seat, hear the clackety-clack of the hooves over the cobbles, see the trickle of water leaking through the roof of the buggy, and relive that burning desire to speak to her. But she kept herself as rigid as a caryatid in the Erechtheion. The constant dripping on my head made me want to sneeze, but I couldn't get out of its way because my mother wouldn't let me move. I did sneeze. "You little freak . . . you're going to catch another cold."

My mother's classical profile, defined by her perfect forehead and chin, contorted into a sneer. She was only twenty-five, but I wondered what she had been like when she was young.

The truth is that youth came to her only once in life but I banished it at a stroke. When she frowned, wrinkles sank rails across her plains, rails along which ran the train of worry. I was its passenger, the cause of the furrows that eroded her beauty until wearing it away like an alfalfa butterfly caught in a pampas gale.

Her favorite was Lula, her youngest daughter. The chubby blond, a sweet child whom she protected all her life, and whom I bullied whenever I had the chance. My mother sang to her firm-fleshed doll, Maria Salomé, Lulita; they even stole those names from me, foisting the name Maria Micaela on me like an ill-fitting coat; at my tender age it had a bitter taste. As the firstborn, I should have had my mother's names, but she held them back to give to her second daughter. And to cap off my sorrows, I wasn't pretty.

I was rebellious and my mother hit me, but I punched back harder without having to raise a finger. Welts formed on the arms I raised to protect myself, inspiring me to invent maladies in an attempt to fit into a scene from which I had already been exiled.

I persisted with the act; or perhaps it was the pain in my soul manifesting itself as mendacious complaints, "I have a headache" or "My feet are cold."

But it was in vain; my witchy mother could sniff out the lie and a malevolent, manic cackle coursed through me that even now reappears at times of stress, as though I were laughing through the throats of ten women.

Back to the photo, I'm still in the buggy. We got out and in the photographer's studio I was placed next to a small table on which sat the basket. "Pretend you're picking up a flower," the man instructed, with the added plea, "Smile." But he couldn't get anything out of me. My arm poked out from my body like the branch of a weeping willow and I was incapable of smiling. My face resembled more the mask of tragedy, pouting and grimacing. My mother's eyes gleamed horribly when she realized that the photograph would be a fiasco.

The kindly photographer adjusted a pleat on my dress and said, "Look here, little girl, here comes the birdie." I was mollified and began to giggle; I thought the situation ridiculous.

"I'm telling your father when we get home," my mother threatened. "Do what you can with the little freak," she said to the man in a resigned voice.

My mother knew that she could never tame me, she knew without my ever saying a word that I found the idea of having my photograph taken stupid, that I could already read and write in spite of my youth, that I started to read road signs and numbers at the age of three without anyone having taught me. I treated them, the grown-ups, as I saw fit, I made fun of them, I hated them. She knew that I was far superior to other children my age and that I would be the downfall of both her and her favorite daughter. She was afraid of me, and I knew it.

It had stopped raining by the time we left the dark studio. Golden sunlight was flooding down, warming the well-marshaled flowers on Plaza San Martín, the lime trees and the magnolias.

The sun lent a golden sheen to my mother's silk dress, which was chestnut with little painted swirls and a pleated skirt. Her high-heeled boots were brown and on her head she wore an Italian sun hat, which did nothing to detract from the proud, bronzed skin of a true Argentine woman. She was carrying a plush suede purse, soft as Lula's skin. The downside, the only ugly thing about her, was what she was dragging along, Chela, Maria Micaela Stradolini, her skinny, dark firstborn, who was nothing but a big pair of eyes.

In the cafés, children with far greater freedom than I lapped up ice creams, cones of chocolate and red and pink fruit. No one was supervising them and at the counters they carried themselves like self-assured dwarves while I dangled from my mother's hand like a furious puppet. I'd have sold my soul for a lick of freely obtained ice cream, but she went to Confitería La Perla for her tea and dry cookies. I hate tea and dry cookies.

I could hear the joyful burble of the free in the street. My imagination was beholden to images of their multicolored cones while the waiter neatly laid out our order on the tablecloth embroidered with the name of the establishment.

After "Confitería La Perla," I read out the labels on the jars, the boxes on the shelves, and the brands of sweets while my mother simmered with rage.

The teapot and kettle steamed, the cookies on the little plate made the atmosphere sugary and syrupy.

Pretending to be stupid, I went on reading labels to demonstrate my distaste for the outing. She read my mind. "Ice cream makes bronchitis worse."

My bronchial lobes were like a spluttering engine, but what harm could an ice cream do to what was already a chronic sickness? Mother poured the tea. "Come on, eat."

She savored the English delicacy but I've always found it bland.

My lonely seagull eyes flew over the solidified water of her diamond ring, across a hostile, miserly sea, the dark waters down below, the ebony beads of her double necklace, her golden earrings.

"Mother, why have you never loved me, not even a little?"

She pointed at my cup. "Your tea's getting cold."

The column of steam no longer spiraled up from the porcelain depression, it had been defeated by my stubbornness. I swirled it around twice, like when I cleaned my teeth, and swallowed the disgusting liquid. She ate her cream cookies and the twisted, crunchy palmera pastries while sugared music sweetened the air, the sound of my childhood, evoking images of Charlie Chaplin: "La Violetera." Shy flowers danced on lilac-blue legs up graceful columns toward a fin de siécle ceiling painted in a naive Baroque style, with ingenuous round capitals and a honeyed rose garden.

1925, when La Plata, the capital of the Province of Buenos Aires, was still a paradise. We'd traveled in from our nearby estate just to take the photo to send to Aunt Angelina, a relative of my father's, in Italy. Idyllic times, in spite of the bitterness wrought and cast my way by the other members of the household.

My legs danced under the table, silly as Chaplin's, a madcap dance that if performed in public would make the audience laugh, just as much as they did at the unfortunate Chaplin with his tragic shoes that helped him to flee down long roads after playing the fool.

Watching his films at the cinema upset me. I was a Chaplinesque girl, clumsy and comical. When I was four, I decided that the actor was my spiritual brother.

I am still wounded today by the mimed dialogues, the loving feelings and advances expressed with just a flutter of the eyelashes and contorted eyebrows, the sorrow of the little mustache stuck like a chocolate onto his upper lip, the aristocratic buffoon who embodied the baldness of the skull better than Hamlet. The family remarked on my long, ñandu-chick limbs and my enormous feet, which were as much of a burden to me as Chaplin's shoes must have been to him.

Mother remained unmoved—she kept her anger bottled up inside—at my lack of appetite, although I nibbled hungrily at my nails.

"Pig . . . you like that, do you? I'm going to put caca on your nails so you enjoy them even more." She knew how to put on a performance. Some gentlemen called out a compliment, "What a doll." She just blushed a little. The men must have thought their doll was urging me to try the cream pastries: *Eat, honey, they're delicious.*

She started to put on her gloves. Her hands were those of a failed concert pianist who had sacrificed her career to marry before her little sister. She always had to win. But she always lost.

"You'll see, the moment we get home I'm telling your father about all the trouble you've caused me this afternoon."

What trouble?

Having been tempted into giggling in a photography studio

where I stood stiff as a board and thought the promise of a birdie was stupid and reading out things that were there to be read, of course.

Mother would be getting fat soon. Her pregnancy would bring an end to the tight-fitting dresses, the pleated tube skirts, and tottering around on Louis XV heels.

I already knew where children came from and all the rest although not in great detail. I had simply reasoned it out. My mother thought she was living with a monster.

"Chela is a pest." My two grandmothers could agree on that at least.

They'd argue:

"Lula is as pretty as her mother."

"No, she gets it from the Stradolini side of the family."

The two old women competed over a conventional beauty. A lovely, docile baby.

My nicknames were "Crow" and "Big Nose."

"Shitty old crones," I'd scream at them.

I wanted my future brother to be horrible. Maybe it was a sister. No. I knew it was going to be a nasty boy.

"Lula isn't any trouble, she eats like a little lady."

They didn't say a word about me. It was worse than if they'd called me hateful, surly, smelly.

They didn't deign to use any adjectives at all and the

indifference hurt as though I'd never been born. It was a two-hour trip back to the house in the buggy, and fear stalked me all the way. *I'm telling your father.*

I had put ants in Lula's diapers, mother blamed a careless maid. I drew ugly animals on her mosquito net: reptiles, hippopotamuses, herds of prehistoric beasts, from the bright, colorful pages of *Caras y Caretas*. She cried when I pinched her, or put up with the wasp sting pretending to be asleep. I hated her. I was two years older than my sister and was stubbornly inventing a new enemy.

Even though it was a warm night, I felt cold. It was the kind of cold I only ever got over once in my life. I had a pain in my chest. Similarly, I only ever got over that pain in my chest once in my life. The hinges on the gate creaked and we headed into bitter territory.

My father, as usual, was reading in his study while he smoked his oh-so-dainty meerschaum pipe. His colleagues had just honored him with a promotion. *Maybe he'll be in a good mood*, I thought to myself. Mother kissed him as she came in. "Mama . . . mama," the idiot Lula cried.

"Chela was very naughty."

"Go to your room without supper."

They didn't even bother to tell me off. I threw myself onto the bed and cried. I have shed many tears over my father. Never over her. I wet my pillow with tears of rage, I wanted to die.

In the morning, I invented pastimes to keep me busy, I invested objects with my dreams, I made up characters, I became the proud accomplisher of thousands of feats. My psyche and my soma were harmoniously integrated and wandered through idyllic landscapes, some of them real, some of them fantasy. I didn't like doing chores. Well, I did get great pleasure out of washing mother's fine porcelain and the knickknacks from her display case. I would add a great deal of soap to a large tub, a veritable drift of soapy snow, and used a cloth to clean the delicately carved objects, little stoneware artworks, Murano glass, porcelain from Austria, Germany, and France. My mother loved these mementos. She clung to the dead gilded universes to escape her domestic reality as a failed pianist. I would clean the English pottery, the oriental Buddhas, the gleaming Venetian silhouettes so mysterious with their specks of embedded gold, gondolas from the Lido, sailing over the Adriatic. And in the big soapy tub the landscapes would float around under my scrubbing hands.

"Be careful, they're heirlooms . . . I don't know why you insist on doing that," lamented my mother.

I would rub the cloth over the carvings, the gilt, the tiny signatures that affirmed this or that provenance or ancient date. And after covering them thoroughly in suds, I would wipe clean glasses, little bottles, amphorae, Neapolitan wine flasks whose jeweled blood flowed on, still alive after being emptied like the shell of a firefly. While I did the chore I had chosen for myself,

I fantasized about Europe and Asia, I brought whole continents into the rustic air of the estate. I was already clever enough to read History of Art and Europe was my goal. The supervisor continued to plead, "Careful, they're memories."

I intentionally knocked the odd thing against the edge of the tub, or might carefully allow a glass with a wobbly base to sway back and forth and catch it in midair just as it was about to hit the ground. My mother suffered.

Camelia Obieta, who was something more than my father's friend, would screech, "How can you let the child horse around with the objects from the display case?"

During my chore, I would invent little plays, one of whose titles was *Falsity*, and the protagonist was Camelia Obieta. I couldn't understand why my mother, who knew everything, put up with it. I thought that my mother was as indecent as they were. But sometimes, to reassure myself, I'd reflect that perhaps only I had realized what was going on. Pondering the "Camelia" issue, I washed the lid of a soup dish with a beautiful landscape of the Bay of Naples painted on it. There was Capri, with its ragged trees, the splendid sky over the marina, Santa Lucía and the Roca della Madonna. Suddenly, Vesuvius erupted. I saw great clouds of smoke billow upward and rivers of lava flow downhill, scorching everything in their path, and horrifying ruptures appear in the earth's crust. The lid flew and smashed to pieces.

From a remote shore, I heard the cry of the Gorgons: "When your father gets home."

I froze. I was as bereft as a hero who has lost their sword and shield. A pair of wings like dead leaves sprouted from my heels. I was standing alone at the door to an orphanage, but I didn't cry. I gathered up the ancient fragments, I think that I kissed them. I felt my chest shatter too, and coughed; my bronchial lobes were a pair of sputtering engines.

I'd read about the banquet of the gods and I sat at the table and listened to the clock chimes open the doors of fear; half past twelve, one, half past one, and so on until four o'clock, when my father would arrive.

I lay down on the root of a willow tree. I didn't eat. From where I was, I could hear mother and Camelia's stupid chatter. I had the indecent hope that when my father saw the femme fatale he would forget about me. Lulita was having lunch in the dining room. I peeked in at her and saw a single plate on a pink tablecloth and the silver cutlery that had belonged to mother when she was a girl. Lula used everything like a little lady.

In my childhood, I was never able to eat with cutlery, I ate with my hands to finish more quickly, to just get it over with and start on something else. Chela is a beast, they said, and it didn't bother me. I loved animals, so I didn't see it as an insult. My father would say, "She might be very intelligent, extremely gifted, but she eats like a pig."

Now I was chewing on grass because I was thirsty. My tummy itched and I lifted my shirt; I saw red dots on my skin as though wasps had been at it. I realized that I was sick and was possessed by a savage joy. They'd finally realize I was alive, that I was human enough to get sick, just like other children. The high fever dried out my throat and my eyes began to weep. I fell asleep praying to the gods that it was the black pox.

My father called me.

I woke up. I went to the study. My father was smoking, not reading. He didn't bother swiveling his chair toward me.

"You have done something atrocious, you have broken a collector's piece that my mother, your grandmother, gave to your mother when we married. You have committed a crime against beauty."

In response I let out the peep of an ailing bird.

"Hush, you are bad and devilishly rebellious, you don't act like a daughter of mine or your mother's."

Peeping isn't talking.

My mother and Camelia came in and saw how red I was.

"What's wrong with the girl, why is she so red?"

"Just what I needed, I'm three months pregnant. If it's rubella, woe betide me and the baby . . ."

"Is it measles?"

"She's had it."

"Chicken pox?"

"Rubella!"

"You may not get it."

"I'll lose the child."

I was naked as a celluloid doll and they prodded my bare child's body. I thought they'd gone mad, I was the sick one, why were they worried about their future son?

I was confined to the attic together with Sara; it was where I spent all my illnesses. I sank roots in that attic, roots that would last forever. Through the narrow window I could see the pinkish evening, the same color as the peach jam that was recommended for the sick. Jam on the inside and out, that and the constant feeling that I was going to vomit. Sara brought a potty and said, Vomit. Sara was black and looked as though she was made of rubber. She blended into the shadows of the room and I was left alone in the wreckage.

Sara and the mumps, Sara and the measles, Sara and scarlet fever, Sara and chicken pox, and now back with me along with the seething, burning welts.

Sara and the nightmares that turned the floor into crumbly pastry for strawberry ice cream, or made scraggly scarecrows run across the attic and leap onto my bed, macro-encephalitic dwarves with pointy teeth and eyes like hard-boiled eggs.

I screamed.

"Don't be scared, it's the fever."

The doctor came. "Let's take a look at your tongue, my girl . . ."

The term of endearment moved me. I cried. But the doctor didn't notice because my condition produced tears. I knew, though, that I was crying over the novelty of tenderness.

"Ice cream, doctor, strawberry ice cream . . ."

"Sara, give her an enormous scoop of ice cream, it'll be good for her."

Sara asked after my mother.

"I'm worried about María Salomé, this disease in the third month of pregnancy."

"The poor madam."

"I've advised an abortion, it would be the most prudent course of action. But they're with the priest now and the church wants nothing to do with abortions."

I made deductions from my bed.

I recovered. Like a swamp creature I left my lair and went out into the fields.

Sara began to hate me for what happened to mother. Before, when Sara loved me a little, I bathed. Now I wouldn't take the trouble. I ran through the countryside, my pajamas sticking to my skin. I slid down the banister like a shooting star. My messy braids, tied up with ribbons, bounced off my back. Health was a plant whose roots were nourished by mud, a wild happiness burnished the sky.

The randomly scattered fruit trees began to swell with seeds for another season lurking inside the little apples. There were peach trees, satsumas from the east, pomegranates from the south of Spain, the American grapevines known as "chinche" with their soft, tightly packed bunches, and early plums that dripped their blood onto the paths. On to the next honeyed burst of fig with its sugary, golden tears, I ran through it all, messy and free. Dirty and soiled, I enjoyed unlimited independence. And I climbed trees in the shade, so clean were the willows whose crystalline sap was like tears calling for a green handkerchief to soak in, the upright poplar, the even straighter, elegant cypress. I ran across the fields of Buenos Aires, a carpet burning in places with red and blue thistles like vegetable roosters, across patches of tiny flowers entangled with the clover.

Such were my idyllic meadows.

My great-grandfather loved the sun with Italian passion. He was an agricultural engineer. He knew how to take command because he understood his peasant workers.

He planted the trees himself so his descendants would remember him and follow his example.

I knew him from an oil portrait that still hung in the room where he died.

He left a book of memories. He didn't have a high opinion of the Buenos Aires peasantry. "The criollos are proud and content with their biscuit, mate, asado, and wine. They find it hard to bend their backs," he wrote alongside other similar statements. He asked too much and was not well liked by his workers. To him, the land was a demigod that had to be served and adored every minute of the day or night.

He was laconic as a Doric, frugal as a Stoic.

My father inherited something from this intriguing character, but my father was cruel and I know from experience; cruel and hostile. My father's father, my grandfather, lived in Paris his whole life, spending as much as he could without ever managing to empty the coffers filled by tenacious immigrants. The women of my family were prematurely aged by fear and prejudice. The only thing my maternal ancestors, who were from San Juan, ever planted was the family tree, which wasn't good for anything.

The summer passed and I rediscovered the world. Objects and subjects gave themselves up to me and I perceived new dimensions. I decided to bring order to my surroundings and to put every object and subject in its proper place, in accordance with its nature and importance. I decided to keep my imagination in check. I would reason as logically as possible.

These were my vacations from kindergarten; soon I would go into the first grade. The teacher, who knew about my intellectual abilities, suggested that I go straight into second grade so as not to upset my fellow pupils. "She can't be spending her time in first grade learning how to count with her fingers when she can already read and write and knows her times tables."

That summer, my grandmother from San Juan came to the estate with my cousin Arnaldo. Arnaldo was so white that he blended into the old woman's skirts the way Sara had in the shadows of my attic. The fool wore velvet pants and kept a slingshot in his pocket to fire at birds. The moment he set foot in the garden, he was a threat to the local wildlife. The birds screeched and the dogs howled.

I knew that we would be enemies forever. "He's like a little Englishman," said my grandmother, lifting a pant leg a little to reveal disgustingly pale skin.

"I have creams brought in from Paris, I don't like dark skin, and the boy could get burned in this sun."

The old woman surreptitiously glanced at my coarse, indigenous skin, my unruly hair, the muddy shoes, my generally unkempt appearance. I casually wandered over and hissed into the kid's ear, "Fairy."

My grandmother set out her stall.

"My daughter is going to go through a hard time, the disease you gave her will do its work and nothing good will come of it."

I decided to scandalize them.

"Mommy will get an abortion."

"Children, my dear, come from Paris, or their parents find them in a cabbage patch," the old woman was quick to inform the boy.

"I like the ones that come from Paris better," the boy replied.

"Yes, my love, my darling, they're brought by storks," the grandmother went on.

"Ignorant old woman, storks are Dutch," I corrected her.

I immediately explained to my cousin how babies are born and my grandmother fainted.

When I turned two, my mother was pregnant with Lula. Then a woman came to the house with a leather suitcase. I was messing around out back with spoons and a piece of metal, pretending to play the xylophone.

Someone tried to tell me that my little sister had arrived inside the suitcase but I knew that all it contained was surgical instruments.

I remember when Lula was born, the desperate cry of a creature forced to wake up, obliged to swap serene tranquility for worldly noise, mingling with the notes from the xylophone.

Now, after Lula, another sibling would be born because the priest said, "The will of God must not be crossed," and my family said, "Amen."

A shiver of guilt suddenly swept through me, my hair

stood on end to think of the mystery of my illness and its conse-
quences for the baby. My emotional neglect grew worse when
I turned five. Sara cast me aside. She looked after me during
working hours but only because she had to. I was forbidden to
touch the things in the display case.

I'd steer my life in a different direction. I'd search for treasure under the ground. I read the life and work of Florentino
Ameghino and decided to copy him by hoisting a sack on my
shoulder. Instead of finding extraordinary things, I'd be "the
crazy rag-and-bone girl."

Lying facedown on the earth, I'd scratch holes into it, and
the smell that came out along with the thousand mouths that
opened up to swallow organic matter and give back something
in return explained to me the concept of symbiosis, and I said to
myself that nothing is lost, everything is transformed, conclud-
ing that there is nothing more vivacious and alert than mother
earth, as inert as she might look. My yearning for discovery
was satisfied for the moment by colored stones, pebbles, glass,
roots, and insects dried out by the sun. My skin grew darker
and darker, I became a terra-cotta doll.

Sara would leave a ham-and-cheese sandwich close to my
lair along with a drink that tasted like piss when it got warm.
Sometimes I ate the sandwich but I always wrote a message on
the napkin in which it was wrapped: "The piss is for you."

My cousin began his assault on the local flora and fauna.

He shot at an owl chick. The stone hit the little animal in the wing and the idiot amused himself pulling on the half-torn-off appendage. I swore I would kill him one day.

And, in a way, I did, but much later. The owl was a small, ash-colored chick with cat eyes. I bargained with the horrible boy.

"I'll give you twenty cents for the owl."

"Thirty or I'll kill it."

"I'll give you forty, you degenerate, give it to me."

"Give me the forty cents . . ."

"Give me the chick first."

I tore it off him, the idiot lost his balance, and I trod on his hands. Then I hit him in the head with a stick as hard as I could. He started to cry, calling out for his grandmother.

I slipped away into the long grass with my bird.

"I shall baptize you. Your name is Bertoldo."

I would bring a new inhabitant to the attic, which was already home to a mother cat, her kittens, and the lizard Josefina. They often ate my food, leaving me to peck at the crumbs. They were always hungry whereas I was hungry only sometimes. And as unlikely as it might seem, we had wonderful conversations over the course of magical evenings.

My tenants ran around the attic of the country house, which I pretended was the tower of a castle or a pampas fort overlooking the Portuguese flower farms, and they came at my call or reacted to the different tones of my voice.

"Nobody owns anyone, if you stay it's because you've chosen me."

The mother cat had an argument with Bertoldo and took her children out into the fields. She would come to visit us with them when they were older.

One night we heard a faint gasp. Josefina, who had grown old, died. I buried her at the foot of a rosebush. Bertoldo settled onto the bookshelf, like a lamp, like a tiny lighthouse his head swiveled around eerily, hiding his chestnut beak.

"Hoo . . . hoo . . . hoo . . ." he would greet me.

He learned to climb down the spiral staircase, to fly through the window and wait for me below. We shared whatever food we had and were skinny but very happy. Our souls were well-nourished. I celebrated my fifth birthday with him.

Unfortunately, weakness got the better of me with Sara.

"Sara, what day is it?"

"December 20."

"Doesn't that remind you of anything?"

"It's a day like every other day of the year, December 20, 1926."

I had been trying to weave a bridge of silver thread, or silk like in Japanese prints, between my solitude and the maid but she severed it with scissors. I started to sing, "Maids smell like rotten tobacco." It made her sad and I went on, "I think maids were made from caca and peepee."

And just as I was turning five, I saw her suddenly turn five hundred, get up from her wicker chair, and, weary from ancient bondage, wipe away a tear that glistened on her skin.

My childhood died with Sara.

We would never talk properly again. I had commenced my intellectual period, an age in which I was oblivious to those I scorned, because that was how I had been brought up.

And in spite of my indifferent attitude, one night when I was feeling extremely lonely, I drank mouthwash in an attempt to kill myself. I did it because of Sara, so she would suffer after I died. She stood me in front of the bathroom sink and said, "Vomit." I couldn't, I just gagged. "Put your fingers down your throat and vomit."

I did. My proud attempt at suicide swirled down the drain with no grace or honor. I felt sick for a month, but I didn't complain.

Bertoldo and I were a happy pair of country bums. The idyllic estate offered up untold beauty and finds for the sack, everything from a sunset to a brick engraved with the slogan "Long Live the Blessed Federation," gaucho beads, buckles, flasks, knucklepieces, spurs, and coins, some of them silver, and paddles from old laundries.

We tipped out the sack in the attic. I said to my comrade, "I shall make an addition to 'the crazy rag-and-bone girl': 'the crazy rag-and-bone girl and associates.'" We ventured into a place where there was an abandoned building, we went into rooms with no roof and pockmarked, half-collapsed walls. Dangerous. We climbed the crumbling, damp guard tower. Bertoldo's "Hoo . . . hoo . . . hoo . . ." rang out over the roofs of the farms and the Portuguese crossed themselves. The ruin had a cellar, we went down and found stripped old barrels with their contents spilling out like guts and jugs with a little wine still left in the bottom that had an acid smell. The barrels and jugs gave off the concentrated aroma of extremely old liquor and I realized that we were in a wine cellar. Nearby, we found cow skulls that had been used as seats.

We lifted the red tiles of the patio with a pickaxe. Bugs jumped out that Bertoldo devoured. While I watched him eat the living creatures, I thought of God feeding himself like that, lunching on us indifferently. Without forgetting my natural paganism, I considered the possibility of a single god. Looking around me, I concluded, "It must have been the main building on the estate, the family house."

I said to Bertoldo,

"Why didn't they use the foundations to build a new house?"

"Hoo . . . hoo . . . hoo . . ."

I stomped on the tiles like a marching soldier and Bertoldo hopped from one to another. Suddenly, one gave way. I pushed down hard with my foot to uncover quite a deep hole. I hesitated before shoving my hand in. But then I did, right up to the forearm, and felt something cold but inanimate; it was neither amphibian nor reptile, but had a profile, a little statuette maybe. I took it out and found that it was a sculpture of several figures, very crude, representing a family with monstrously big heads.

I thought of *Las Meninas* by Velázquez.

"They're in the Prado Museum, in Madrid," I told Bertoldo.

"Hoo . . . hoo . . . hoo . . ."

The parents weren't so bad, it was the children who were horrifying.

The sculpture had a piece missing. I would go on looking. I shoved my hand back in, right up to the elbow, and found a metal plaque with the inscription "La Angelina."

A velvety night with a full moon had fallen upon us. It was Friday.

We were afraid and, like Orpheus, we went back to the surface without looking back at the bridge that connects the magical world with the ordinary, everyday realm.

We both, tense and stiff, looked upward at the mystery that hangs like mist between heaven and earth.

As usual, we reentered the house through the servants' entrance and climbed up to the attic by the spiral staircase, our sack full. I was proud at having been brave enough to shove my hand and arm into the abyss. Bertoldo flew to his shelf and

I went to wash in the tub, pouring water from a jug. I didn't use the main bathroom out of fear of meeting the other residents of the house. There was a little bathroom in our attic. The food was on a tray with a glass of the orange drink.

"Are you there?" Sara called out.

"Hoo . . . hoo . . . hoo . . ." I answered.

"Stop playing the fool and come downstairs, your father wants to see you."

In my panic, I lost control of my sphincters and warm urine ran slowly down my leg. I doubled over with a powerful, corrosive stomach ache and sweated from every pore. Freezing like a plant in August, I thought I'd suddenly come down with something. But I obeyed just the same.

My father was reading and smoking as usual. He opened his mustached, bearded maw, sharpened his basalt eyes, folded up the paper, and blew several plumes of smoke. I felt a damned attack of nerves coming on and held back the giggles by biting my nails.

"You have a brother. Your mother gave birth two hours ago."

"Hoo . . . hoo . . . hoo . . ."

"What are you doing?"

The only person who ever spoke to me was Bertoldo. I blushed, because the words "gave birth" made me embarrassed.

"Seeing as you're so intelligent, a freak of learning, I shall simply inform you, like a grown-up, that your mother gave birth."

He had the advantage, as usual, and I saw him inside a red frame and I hated him. A greenish aura filled the room. No love was lost between the Stradolinis.

The red frame around my father fluctuated. And he was inside like a strange image that had nothing to do with me. He was speckled with green blotches. My father wasn't happy about the new baby. My hatred burned brighter.

"I see that you have nothing to say, that you don't care at all. You may leave," he said.

I fled the cave of the bearded/mustached/whiskered major son of a bitch that was my father, and went up the spiral staircase. Back in the attic I lit a candle in the bronze candlestick whose light fell on the small sculpture I had found with a mysterious flicker that made the figures seem to move.

The little people with the big heads were munching on time with their sharp teeth. Bertoldo stared out at everything worriedly. Sara came up for the tray and glass.

"What's my brother's name?"

"Juan Sebastián."

At the edge of the candlelight, which was like delicate embroidery, I said to Bertoldo, pointing at the ugliest figure, "Will he be like that?"

He tilted his little round head and uttered a single "Hoo . . ."

Now a different aura enveloped the attic, something like a lilac cloud floated up and almost touched us. Bertoldo saw it too. In one corner, forgotten and covered in dust, stood my great-grandmother's harp, and it was as though a silken hand plucked it, making what sounded like a wail. I could see, the way you see things underwater, a hand whose fingers were adorned with golden rings, plucking the strings. Bertoldo turned toward it and cooed. I went over to the harp and fingered the strings. I felt a very gentle touch on my hand and the caress continued up to my elbow. I found that it awoke a dormant note of love, family tenderness, and home in my soul.

Unknown experiences long since swept into a corner of my ruined existence began to shimmer for the first time and the hope of some degree of company, warmth, and humanity filled me with a rare pleasure. Yes. There must be a universe for the despairing and abandoned. For the attic creatures. We slept without fear through to the dawn.

I didn't want to see my mother for anything in the world. I'd have given anything not to meet my brother. But I loved the boy's names and chanted them over and over again, "Juan Sebastián, Juan Sebastián." I chanted them in the attic and out in the fields in the light of day, surrounded by cool, fresh alfalfa. I chanted them climbing trees in the shade, the clean willows whose crystal sap is like a weeping person mopping up the tears with a green handkerchief, the tall poplar and the even straighter and more elegant cypress.

As though trying to seed the names in the noble fields, I chanted them running across the vegetable carpet scorched in places by red and blue thistles like crests of feathers, across the patches of little flowers scattered among the clover. I sang "Juan Sebastián" on my estate, my Eden, it was a way of sharing it with someone I hadn't even met yet.

I didn't just share the landscape with Juan Sebastián but also my discoveries: the bricks with messages, the marbles and buckles, the silver coins, the knucklepieces, laundry paddles and endless bones.

It was Bertoldo, the ghost, and I.

We showed the ghost the hole in the old red patio where the sculpture came from and the plaque from ancient Angelina, and the three of us were exiles, bums, vagabonds returning to the surface without looking back across the bridge that united the magical with the ordinary.

The three of us walked stiff and tense, looking up at the waxing, enchanted red moon.

I was studying catechism at the chapel because I had to take my first communion. I was named an assistant to the priest. I won a book on "Sacred History" and was appointed to teach the catechism myself. I found the little moon of unleavened bread in the sacristy intriguing, but overall I wasn't convinced by the fantastical string of stories and tales of which our preparation consisted.

The spinsters who had taught the catechism before me started to get annoyed because the children said I looked amused while I taught and the fusty old women were deadly serious. But although I asked well-intentioned questions that they answered cheerfully, I had to resign because the older children fired spitballs and threw peanuts.

They threw trash and I spat back swear words that stopped them in their tracks. They had no idea what to make of me, I was much fiercer in a fight than the boys. I stood out. I was quietly forgotten. I thought that I had found peace.

The storm was stirred up by Father Luzón. Luzón smelled of yellow soap and cheap cologne, and the old parishioners were crazy about him. *He's a cutie pie*, they said and fought over who got to confess first. He sat in the booth carved like a tiny cathedral and they eagerly went to unburden themselves of their sins.

By the end of the afternoon, Luzón would reemerge looking more dead than alive; weak and pale.

Luzón got upset with me because of the Daughters of Maria and my observations regarding his person. One afternoon, I went into the confessional and smelled a potent aroma

of bleach, similar to a bull in heat. I deduced that Luzón grew
excited by the catechists and masturbated in the booth. *What a
son of bitch, he's always scolding us for our bad deeds and he's just
a major wanker*, I thought. The thought made my blood boil,
causing me problems that I resolved in my own way.

I had to confess to Luzón, who naturally asked, as he did
all the children,

"My girl, have you committed any bad deeds? Did you do
them alone, or with others?"

I had already argued with the Daughters of Maria about
masturbation and immaturity. I lacked emotional urges, I had
never experienced love, my sex was smothered by my extraordinary intellectual gifts. I had often seen boys masturbating
and considered it natural and so ignored it. In the chapel, they
said it was a mortal sin.

In a quiet but piercing voice, I answered Luzón,

"What you call bad deeds are normal at a certain age, but
what you do when your parishioners turn you on is disgusting."

One of the catechists, Miss Masselotte, was assigned to talk
to my father.

"It pains my soul, but tomorrow at four in the afternoon, I
shall go to see your father."

I decided to give her pain somewhere more tangible than
her soul.

Juanín Big Gun, the madman, brandished his enormous

penis. Juanín lay back in the grass, offering passersby his only treasure. *Show us, show us*, the boys would encourage him. The girls would pretend to be scandalized, *Look how big it is. Touchy, touchy*, Juanín would call out.

To different degrees, Juanín and I suffered from the same problem: he had no intellect but was one hundred percent emotion, and I was the opposite. We were both freaks. We ought to have died, or been put out of our misery. We were a pair of degenerate oddities, and that made us natural targets for the normal.

Crazy old Juanín was always hungry so I called him over, waving my ham-and-cheese sandwich, whispering, "Masselotte touchy, touchy."

One spoke to Juanín the same way as they would speak to an animal. He understood me, wolfed down the food, and stood ready, penis in hand.

I leaned into his ear. "I'll give you more if . . ."

"Masselotte touchy, touchy," I sang.

Masselotte came down the hill along Laid Back Juanín's— his thing was so big it warrants capital letters—path.

He jumped up like a rattlesnake and Masselotte was knocked over. Juanín ran his splendid offering the length of the hypocrite's body, not forgetting her face and hair, and covered every inch of her with his spray.

From among the thistles, I called out, "You're not ashamed

to commit bad deeds with innocent Juanín Big Gun, you spin-ster whore, I'm telling your boyfriend, Father Luzón."

She fled the field as guiltily and scruffily as a recently de-spoiled youth.

None of the catechists or catechumens ever saw her again. *She must have gone to hide in a catacomb somewhere*, I said to myself. And at that moment I swore to myself that I would win all my wars, whatever it took. I would be determined and guilt-free. I had no reason to love my neighbor if my neighbor hated me. But if I was so different, who was my peer?

Mother lived in Buenos Aires with Juan Sebástian. My fa-ther stayed in La Plata almost every day. Sara spent all her time looking after Lulita, but she still sewed my first communion dress and bought the shoes and gloves.

Luzón was avoiding me. I would take my communion without confessing. It wasn't as though I was a believer.

On December 8, I dressed in white. Sara helped me into the dress and draped the lace of hope. Suffocating inside the silk tube and choking on the lace, I was a fly in milk. *Damn it*, I cursed as I forced feet more accustomed to slippers into shoes. Sara had dressed me up as a mosquito net.

"If you don't believe in God, why are you taking communion?"

"I won a book on 'Sacred History' . . ."

"You may know about religion, but you don't believe in God."

I picked up the rosary and strode away.

"As you can see, your mother didn't give you the gold rosary, she's saving it for Lulita."

My ivory rosary had belonged to Aunt Angelina Stradolini de Caserta, one of my father's Italian aunts, which is why they took the photograph of me that stormy day.

Back then, Angelina was just an ivory rosary.

Who knows what nonsense Sara was mumbling. I pushed her away and ran to the chapel.

Stumbling through the weeds, she called out, "You're very bad, God will punish you."

She followed on behind, doing her best to protect my lace train from the brambles, sobbing quietly.

I could already hear the girls' chorus, *Oh, holy altar / protected by angels / I come to you / for the first time.*

Would Masselotte venture out from her hiding place?

She wasn't there, but a close friend of hers took advantage of a quiet moment to declare, "Stradolini is the ugliest." She was right. I looked like a long-legged rhea chick, but this was no place for immature fowl.

Big birds don't need to take communion. I was struck by a fit of the giggles. Tears came to my eyes as I struggled to keep from laughing.

When I was given the consecrated bread, I couldn't stand it anymore, the giggles welled up inside me, I almost choked.

When the parents kissed their daughters, I realized that I had never been kissed.

I abruptly stood up in my pew, and a devilish splinter caught what was left of my lace train. It ripped with a little screech.

"Freak," Sara exclaimed.

Feeling the need to elaborate, she added, "She's very clever at her studies but for everything else she's good for nothing. At home we call her the Freak."

More than a communion, it was a second baptism or confirmation. Sara had rechristened me "Freak." I could have killed her.

I was enrolled in school with a forged birth certificate dated 1917 and by eight years old, when most children were just starting out, I was in the sixth grade. I got straight As in every class and Fs in behavior. The teachers sighed in relief when, halfway through the year, I was moved up a grade. My rise from class to class was so swift that I didn't have time to make friends.

My isolation flourished like a tropical vine. I ate with the animals, which is to say Bertoldo and the creatures of the field, leaning against the wall while I finished the book I'd started that morning or went over theorems and arguments. I never used cutlery. I might have dated boys but the "Freak" business isolated me still further.

I heard that Mother had returned from Buenos Aires with Juan Sebastián.

My attic over the "people house" was a refuge now that I was afraid of coming across my mother and little brother. When I got back from my adventures with Bertoldo, I hid up there.

I stayed completely silent. I assumed that meeting them would be awful; cold, wild, and violent. I was avoiding horror of some kind. I couldn't say precisely what it consisted of but something terrible lurked in the people house, it throbbed in and out, throwing me off balance.

I immersed myself in the worlds of Math and Logic, the paradises and shades of Plato's *Dialogues*. I wove my enlightened universe out of threads of illustrious lineage, I aspired to a distinctive death, something out of the ordinary that would etch my notable memory in the minds of others.

Oh, yes . . . a death like Rilke's.

And because nothing was denied to my intellect, I learned French and Italian to perfection. I adored Madame de Noailles and the beautifully illustrated collection entitled *Vita dei Animali*, which had belonged to my great-grandfather. I took it up to the attic.

I used the time that normal people waste washing, preening, breakfasting, lunching, drinking tea, having dinner, and all those other commitments and occupations, or whatever you want to call them, to study and enrich myself.

I had a mentor and psychologist, Maria Assuri. She probed me with her gray eyes and wrote down her observations and thoughts about me in her notebook until someone from the house suggested that she accompany me to a private institution.

In March, I would enter said school for my secondary studies. But there was still a good stretch of summer ahead of us. I would choose the books I wanted to take to the institute: Rilke, Romain Rolland, Gide, Proust, and Wilde. Also, the French poets Rimbaud and Baudelaire, French magazines from the past century, and the novels of Benito Lynch, who lived in La Plata and was a friend of my father's.

When Maria Assuri arranged my admittance (and hers), the people in the house became of secondary importance because I had decided to bring an end to the present cycle. One way of burning my bridges was to write my autobiography in two San Martín exercise books, which I would burn immediately. I thought that a fiery catharsis would set me free.

"Now that Lulita doesn't need me anymore, I'll look after the boy," Sara announced.

I still hadn't met my little brother.

Clambering up onto the roof of my attic like a monkey, I looked down on the gardens and the passages but I never saw my mother or the boy. The only thing in my life that even resembled a burden was Bertoldo. I wondered who would love him when I was gone and decided that it would be best for Bertoldo if he died.

I checked his life expectancy in the *Vita dei Animali*. He

stood on the page, casting a shadow on the text, fixing his warm
eyes on my putative cruelty. I explained myself at length, sharing my reasoning, telling him about the nature of the people in
the house, and he understood and grew old. To make up for my
insidious actions, I would take him outside more regularly. We
wandered through the tall alfalfa, along golden paths of dried
fallen leaves that crunched under our feet. Bertoldo flew to the
top of a pine and a willow with its unforgettable, breathtaking
shower of green. We enjoyed the resinous smell of forest fires
that started out small but grew, leaving strips of chestnut, tar-
nished gold, and charcoal in their wake.

These fires are fairly common in January and February and
can be caused by something as insignificant as a shard of glass
or a stray cigarette butt. The smoke floating across the different
parts of the estate stuck to your skin and made your eyes water.
We were sorry for the trees, innocent victims of carelessness
maybe, with their dramatic pitchfork farewells, their skinny
arms trying to beat out the flames, and the giants that survived
the scorching and were soon energetically pushing tender green
shoots from the damaged bark. Perhaps La Angelina had been
consumed by a fire like this that had got out of control?

Perhaps the building had its roofs burned away, leaving the
weathered walls still standing and the red tile patios where sinister forms grieved over the damage from the next world . . .

The patio of discovery . . .

The dark mouth of the hole gaped before me in the middle of the patio. It bothered me as though I could hear it mocking my impoverished appearance and even my feathered companion, so I gave it a kick. A piece of nearby tile went flying. I went on kicking and the crumbling, rotted material fell away, making the hole bigger.

"This is a clever hole," I said to Bertoldo.

Its jagged teeth nibbled at our bodies and the night around us.

The jalopy braked, crushing the clover. The little car belonged to one of the Italian farmers, Don Narciso Gemmi, and he offered to give us a ride.

"Is this where La Angelina's house used to be?" I asked him.

"I think so. They knocked this part down in 1868. This is where your great-grandfather used to live."

"Did you know him?"

"My grandfather did."

We got into the car, sitting on green leather seats on our way to the people house, to our attic. We arrived. We started to climb the spiral staircase into exile. Bertoldo flew to his shelf, I picked up the tales of Hoffman. I read "The Sandman" out loud. Bertoldo blinked as though he'd got sand in his big eyes. The sandman tortured animals with pins and needles. I thought of Maria Assuri; I was an insect stuck with her pins in a display case, which she probed with her gray eyes, keeping me still, classifying, labeling: "Extremely gifted adolescent; problems with basic socialization and other issues." I consoled myself with the idea that abnormal people don't live long. Juanín Big Gun had died at the end of the previous summer.

Sara delivered a message. "Your father says that you shall be eating dinner with the family, Miss Maria Assuri is coming to visit."

The Report

I can't get the image of Luis's face, resurrected from the grave by the power and grace of his loving second wife, out of my mind. For some reason it makes me think of the Aztec flower. But enough irony, I must accept it as a moment of sublimity, as painful as it was. From my personal tomb—the chest of the past—I retrieve the report written by Maria Assuri:

> I hope that Chela understands how much damage her brazen rudeness, her excessive need to be superior, and her abnormal gifts can do to her. I think it will benefit her to be apart from her family. The severe regime at the Institute

might perhaps make her see the value of living in the familial home.

The girl—now an adolescent—is like a difficult-to-pilot ship. Personally, I believe that she is a strange, sadistic creature. I say this because she does whatever she can to exacerbate any given circumstance and make it worse still. I try to observe her without her noticing but it comes as a shock to find that I am the one being observed, and with greater perspicacity and aggression. It knocks me off balance. I'd like to strike some chord of emotion within her, her psyche, soul, or whatever. Chela lacks a sense of feeling for her fellow human beings and loves only animals.

Right now, she knows that she must come down to the "people house," as she describes the lower floors, and I hear her reading, shouting out loud, a page from Romain Rolland. To an owl. I don't recognize Chela's voice in the manly roar.

The girl really is unpleasant; she makes every effort she can to be offensive. She's dirty

with a filthy mouth. Does that voice belong to
Chela? Or has someone or something terrible
taken possession of her? As a scientist, I do not
believe in demonic possession. Inside Chela
lurk intense feelings of hatred and resentment.

I saw her return from her wanderings.

Sara passed on her father's order to come
downstairs; she should have been washing up
but she was reading instead:

> Everyone, deep down within, car-
> ries a small cemetery of those he has
> loved. They sleep there for years and
> years undisturbed. But there comes a
> day when the tomb is reopened and
> the dead rise out of their graves and
> smile with pale lips, lovers forever
> answering their beloved's call, in
> whose breast they sleep like a child in
> their mother's womb.

I spied through a gap in the door and saw
her talking to the owl. I couldn't help but feel
the hair on my skin stand on end when I heard,

"Although we can't see each other with the eyes on our faces, we shall see with the eyes we both know and shall return from the ashes to be what we are and walk together."

I needed to put a stop to this.

"Chela, you must get dressed and come down."

"What? Am I naked?"

Ignoring the angry devil, I found a pair of shoes in the rack and shined them, inviting her to put them on. All I got in return was

> *Life is only a part . . . of what?*
> *Life is only a sound . . . of what?*
> *Life is just a dream of a dream,*
> *but the truth is elsewhere.*

"That's from a poem by Rilke, isn't it, Chela?"

"You're too sociable, ma'am, you wouldn't understand Rilke. The most you can do is mumble verses, nothing more."

I left the attic. Some time later she came down, still dirty, still looking a mess. Did she feel a

hint of emotion when she looked at her father?
Perhaps something akin to an emotion, because
Mr. Stradolini was looking quite diminished.

The father said,

"I know these formalities bother you, but
you'll be leaving here soon. It's best that you
learn of recent developments."

Mr. Stradolini waited for a reply, a question that might demonstrate the girl's interest.
But no.

The father went on,

"You've just turned nine, but with the
forged certificate we've added four more years,
which makes thirteen in all, enough for you to
be admitted to the Religious Institute for your
secondary studies. You and Juan Sebastián are
my disgrace. Two monsters is too many for
one father."

I saw something stir inside Chela, something dark, like a guilt complex. The father
continued,

"After all, you can do what you like with
your life, if you want to attend the Institute,
then do, if you'd prefer a different school say
so, or continue dedicating your life to vagrancy

as you've done so far with that filthy fowl, you little piglet."

I stepped in.

"Very intelligent children are unusual. I've never had a pupil as intelligent as Chela."

There was no love lost in the Stradolini household. Perhaps Chela was the heart of the problem and when she left the situation would improve.

The mother came in with Lula, but not the brother I imagined Chela was hoping to meet. My pupil's slatternly appearance was in stark contrast to that of the other two females.

"The brilliant tend to get distracted and ignore etiquette," I said.

They gave all their attention to Lula. Chela lost whatever poise she still maintained. Things got worse when the food arrived, stuffed turkey. Chela didn't know how to use cutlery. When she tried to fork a morsel, it went flying.

"She may be as intelligent as you say, but she acts like a beast at the table," the father said.

"Like a freak," Lula interjected.

"That can be corrected," I replied.

They all went silent.

Chela didn't eat a bite or say a word and I realized that she had never been part of a family conversation. She intentionally created this state of affairs, clashing with her parents whenever she could. After dessert was served, she threw away her napkin and escaped to her attic. Mrs. Stradolini shed a couple of tears and soon forgot about the incident.

I went up to the attic. Chela was going through her belongings and ripping up papers, as though she wanted to sever any ties she might have had to the past. I never saw a girl who acted so like a gypsy, and if her features weren't so similar to her mother's and her temperament something I judged to have been inherited from her father I would have assumed that she was adopted or had been forced upon the family group but never properly assimilated.

She planned a schedule designed to maximize her time. (A) She would spend the morning out in the fields looking for objects. (B) In the afternoon she would read, write, and

think. (C) At night she would destroy anything useless, even if it was dear to her. Point C
concerned me. The only thing that was dear to
Chela was her owl. A cruel notion tormented
me and I decided to keep watch, to spy if necessary. One night, I heard the little animal sneeze
like a hen with a cold and saw Chela feeding
it a powder dissolved in water, something like
aspirin. After a weighty, gray, leaden silence,
it fell to the attic floor. Chela scurried out of
the attic, as was her way, carrying a small
bundle, and I watched her through the small
window as she went down the slope and buried something at the foot of the rosebushes. I
remembered that other small animals had also
disappeared. Our situation would grow much
more fraught if the girl had decided that she
had a right to kill. As a scientist, I could not
risk an opinion without further research. From
the moment of the burial, I began to feel a deep
aversion, a disgust for the odd creature.

Before leaving the attic, I gathered a number of her texts. I read, "The butterflies have
dried in the wind and the landscape bids me
farewell. Why did I grow up? I didn't ask to

be born. I shall not allow myself to be cowed by the society of so-called normal people; if I do not develop into an ordinary person then all the worse for them . . . I am an extraordinarily gifted animal cast by mistake into a world of common people. I am a zoomorphic deity. My father says that I'm a beast, and he's right. Now I shall leave them in their filthy peace, which stinks of cooking spices, to dine on fine china and use difficult cutlery; they know more about that than I do. I don't have anyone to talk to because Bertoldo will be dead soon and he knows it. He's grown glum and quiet. I'm a beetle lying on my back. I shall make the enormous effort to flip myself over. Before leaving Hell, I shall speak."

I pondered the death of the owl. I felt sick. What poisons did she have access to? If she could poison the only thing she loved, what was she capable of doing to Lula whenever the urge took her? I was stricken with foreboding, which was not at all a psychological attitude. Chela called me to help her wash in the small sink because she didn't want to use the bathroom in the people house. I was afraid that she would notice how nervous I was.

It is hard work to clean a long, albeit skinny realm that has rarely felt the touch of a sponge. Naked and covered in foam, she was like a sexless doll, a young, skinny, prepubescent tomboy. It was an effort to comb her long hair, which reached down to her waist but fell in waves due to having been tied up in braids so often. By the end, while she kept her mouth shut, she was a pleasant little girl. I shan't say pretty, but possessed of some grace. Or a naughty little boy with very dark skin. Someone lost in the jungle, who had never been to a hairdresser.

She started to modulate the timbre and tone of her voice, making sure that it wasn't too deep or shrill. After striking her flag of solitude, she would read Proust as compiled in editions of the *Revue des Deux Mondes* collected by her grandfather. From her lofty intellectual tower, she hoped to overcome the neglect of her relatives. I read the magazine over her shoulder. There was an image of the

"House of Madame Noailles" and a caption by Proust underneath:

> *Come with me to the garden*
> *to see whether the vines have budded,*
> *to see the grasses of the valley.*
> *My garden has orchards*
> *where pomegranate mingles with the*
> *most beautiful fruit;*
> *hedges, tuberose, saffron,*
> *cinnamon, nutmeg, myrrh,*
> *and all manner of scented trees.*

"Perhaps the beautiful, distinguished Madame de Noailles, keeper of orchards, was like a queen with whom Marcel was intellectually enamored?" Chela wondered.

"Hirondelle d'argent," she sighed.

Turning to look at me, she asked,

"Tell me, shall I ever become a silver sparrow?"

"Perhaps," I answered, a little fearfully.

"Do you know who Madame de Noailles was?"

"Yes, I've heard some poems."

She echoed a thought I'd already had:

"Do you think that from my intellectual tower I shall overcome the neglect of the people?"

I didn't know what to answer my nine-year-old specimen.

She asked again about the silver sparrow.

"You aren't being honest with me, I shall never be beautiful like Madame de Noailles, I shall never glow like 'une hirondelle d'argent.'"

The conversation perplexed me. Chela seemed sleepy and fixed her dreamy attention on the magazine. I was almost able to follow her flight of imagination: she soared away from the ugly little rascal she had been and the lair in which she lurked like an animal toward the home of the writer in Chambéry to converse with dignitaries, wandering eighteenth-century terraces among lovely towers and parks rigorously landscaped in the French manner.

Suddenly, she exclaimed,

"I'd wipe away this wild estate with a giant eraser, all that shimmering blue, and draw in its place the leaden tint 'de la champagne' rolling over the rust-colored fish in the ponds."

"Chela, with your voice so beautifully controlled, you should go to the people house and have them listen to you," I ventured.

"I'm not afraid of them, I'll go down."

As she walked down the stairs, I saw her progressively lose her nerve. By the time she got to her father, she didn't say a word.

"You shall go to the Institute with Sara in Narciso's car. Get your things ready, I'll send a trunk up to your hovel."

I believe that Mr. Stradolini was tough and inflexible but how else should he have treated this horrendous scarecrow and her insolent gaze?

I went up to the attic and we looked out through the window. Autumn had just begun. The falling leaves were blocking the gutters, and the rain and the damp brought up an unhealthy stink from the puddles, a scent that clung to you like filthy lace. We packed books, papers, notepads, and junk into Chela's sailor sack, the one she had used for her discoveries.

We set out at six in the morning and began to see the girls when we were a few blocks from

the Institute, some walking, others in cars.
Chela was expressionless, betraying no emotion. I was more excited than she was. The
nuns took attendance in the courtyard. Some
of them peered out, recognizing existing pupils and identifying new faces; students who
had come through the application process had
certain advantages over those sent from other
schools. Sara and Narciso unloaded the trunk
and drove off. Chela observed the girls who
didn't want to leave their mothers, whether
with scorn or envy I don't know. Some cried.
When she got to Chela's name on the list, the
principal nun said, "Oh, the gifted one." We
heard amused giggling in the courtyard. Chela
seethed with fury. She sneezed three times, as
though she had a cold. One of the girls remarked, "At least she sneezes like everyone
else."

"You will be sharing a suite with Analía."

Analía was a petite society blond. She picked
up her suitcases and lithely carried them to the
first floor. Chela was walking a little clumsily
on account of her shoes. She held out her hand

when Analía leaned in to kiss her hello. And when we opened Chela's trunk, there was a minor stampede in the apartment, everyone was eager to see what the freak had brought.

They expected a host of spirits, rabbits, lizards, and gnomes to leap out of the open trunk, but all there was were unfashionable clothes Sara had bought at the Turkish store.

Chela couldn't have cared less. Analía started to unpack a genuinely lavish wardrobe crafted by foreign dressmakers, which even included a party dress.

"You didn't bring a party dress?"

"You're planning on dancing here?"

"Hey, where did you come from? Simple, are you?"

Chela couldn't be honest with these people. She couldn't tell her fellow pupil where she'd come from because she wouldn't have been believed. I realized with sorrow that Chela had brought her exile with her. In their very first conversation, Analía called Chela "simple." She was quite right. Chela is a brilliant simpleton. (Juan Sebastián is an imbecilic simpleton.) She wouldn't be able to stand this ordinary high school community for long. In truth, the human grouping where she would fit in didn't exist. And there she was, standing in the bedroom of a shared suite, uninterested in the luxuries that Analía was parading for her benefit.

I shall compare her to a spider. One of those small spiders that live in flaking walls and sit still until some naughty child bothers them. Then they get angry and pounce. Poison built up inside Chela. Her stay at the Institute didn't last long, partly because she was unable to adapt and partly due to the nature of the place, which was suitable only for normal adolescents. My brilliant simpleton required a different approach.

There is a sufficient number of subjects like Chela for the state to found schools for the extremely gifted. Let the cry ring out. Schools for the gifted. They are the most unfortunate of the abnormal because they understand their situation and are thus more unhappy than the subnormal, who are quite contented with their lives. In her classes and examinations, Chela obtained nothing but straight As. And the envy of her fellow pupils. Twelve- and thirteen-year-olds, some as old as fifteen, beaten by a nine-year-old.

The gifted girl would finish her test and, out of sheer boredom, move onto those of her entire row. The other pupils would surreptitiously pass her their blank pages. Then she'd yawn ostentatiously to show off. I repeat that Chela was never able to be honest with this community but it was impossible to conceal the fact that she had an unusual background in which she had been marginalized. She had no idea about contemporary fashions, not just in terms of clothing but also vocabulary and the formalities with which girls of her age addressed one another. Chela, whose manners were seemingly primitive and instinctive but in fact richly cultured, found it impossible to bear.

Analía especially took advantage of her abilities. "Today, we shan't study history, María Micaela will save us with her chatter," and Chela would delightedly plunge back into the time of Pericles, as though she'd lived in Athens. She liked to teach, to show how ancient wars had played out on maps. The teacher dubbed her "Herodota" and Chela shivered because she knew the burden that a nickname could be. Some of her teachers didn't call on her for answers, others skipped her in roll calls. At staff meetings, they decried her as a "pedant" and the nuns kept watch on the potential succubus from afar.

"Why don't her parents come to visit?"

The Mother Superior was determined to open a breach in the walls so as to unleash a tear or some other kind of humor that might indicate that a girl who barely left the library, didn't like physical exercise, and didn't know how to dance was still human.

She repeated the question,

"Why don't they come to see you?"

"I don't know, ma'am."

"Call me Mother."

She didn't.

"You're isolated, you're not joining in with the others, are you uncomfortable?"

"No."

The nun, visibly irritated by her insouciance, grabbed her rosary.

"You should integrate, converse."

"Is that a school rule?"

"What do you know about the rules?"

"I know them very well. I've read them all and it doesn't say anything about integration."

"Well, I'm in charge here and you will integrate."

Chela smiled mischievously. The nun sent for Analía. Then she sent for Chela's father and waited in vain. The Mother Superior mandated that Chela be docked a grade in every class for refusing to integrate and that she be failed in physical education. Nonetheless, Chela decided to spend her vacation at the school. The Mother Superior sent for me and subjected me to an inquisition worthy of a nun: nothing very deep or important was said but I realized that she believed Chela to be a disruptive element and would find a pretext to get rid of her.

"She doesn't want to leave for vacation. She'd rather prepare, with your assistance, for two years of free study, which it is very unlikely she'll be granted," she said.

I answered that I was happy to stay with

the child during her vacations and would try
to dissuade her from her plans for free study.

I knew that I wouldn't get anywhere;
Chela was a girl of very fixed opinions.

It was a three-month sacrifice for me,
spending whole days in the library with brief
breaks to eat, nothing more. Seeing how excited
she was, almost happy, I didn't dare tell her that
her request would be denied. But perhaps she
sensed it? She didn't react when the denial came.
For three months she only talked about and in-
teracted with books. The sister librarian soon
became familiar with how she spoke to books,
how she treated them, and the work Chela gave
her climbing up and down the ladder.

The girls returned with the glow of summer and love on their skin. In addition to going to the beach, they had found boyfriends.
They gossiped about what had happened on
the outside, giggling and squealing. While the
smell of the sea and magic of the mountains
flowed in the conversations of the recently arrived teenagers, Chela considered her rejected
request, coming to the conclusion that there

was no chance of hope or favor in these surroundings. She decided that that year Analía
would not have the benefit of her learning. The
sociable little witch caught on and set the gears
in motion for a cold war.

"The Mother Superior has summoned me
to report on a certain little person."

Analía was the daughter of minor gentry.
She called them "gentry" because they owned
a few fields and animals. They knew María
Micaela's family. By now, Analía knew more
about them than Chela, even what happened
behind closed doors at the Stradolini house.

I noticed that Chela was eating well, freely,
and ignoring the winks and expressions from
her schoolmates. She was pondering what
Analía was going to say.

She considered a list of potential irreg-
ularities: a failure to integrate, mocking of
the poor and ineffective teachers, keeping
Greco-Roman nudes in her notebook, possession of *Deux Mondes* magazines, smoking.

"What are you going to snitch to the nun
about me?"

"Not snitching, just the pure and unvarnished truth."

"You idiot . . ."

The sister preceptor interrupted,

"You, María Micaela, are guilty of the sins of vanity and pride."

"There are worse sins, such as soliciting betrayal."

"What are you insinuating?"

"Ask the Superior."

"You mean Mother Superior?"

The preceptor was sweating. It beaded comically in her little mustache.

"Dry the sweat from your mustache," Chela brayed.

The fat preceptor nun dried her mustache and ran off in tears. Before she left the room, she spat back at Chela,

"You're an animal."

They successfully executed a plan long in the works . . . Breaking into Chela's apartment and removing *The Songs of Maldoror*, *A Season in Hell*, *The Enlightenments*, *Les Fleurs du Mal*, the collection of French magazines, a full note-book, and two packs of cigarettes.

They summoned Mr. Stradolini, who delegated the duty to Sara.

It was the middle of the school year and preparations were already being made for the Spring Ball, boxes of dresses were arriving, some of whose labels read "Paris-Rome." Gifts for the Institute were being delivered.

I learned that that year she would not be given the academic award due to the reduction in her grades and the fail in physical education. I asked for a meeting with the Mother Superior because Chela wanted to talk to her. It was arranged.

"Ma'am, when will you be returning my books, my nudes, my magazines, and my cigarettes?"

I wanted the earth to swallow me up.

The nun clutched the beads of her rosary.

"You little devil . . . This is why you asked for a meeting, Miss Assuri? You should know that you shan't be here next year."

Sara came that afternoon. She spoke to the Superior and left without seeing us.

With the ball approaching, on Analía's bed shimmered a yellow organdy dress with ribbons at the chest and a bee's nest at the yoke.

"Do you like it?" she asked Chela.

"Snitch."

Analía tried to scratch her but Chela bent her double with a kick to the stomach.

"What rubbish did you tell the nun about me?"

"You're as crazy and degenerate as your dwarf brother, you're both rotten, or do you think I don't know?"

I saw that Chela was taken aback by the news. And then came more: "Your mother is pregnant and she'll have another nut." This was too much for me to contain. Chela was as strong as a wild beast suddenly let loose from its cage. She pushed me away and fell upon Analía. I heard the ominous crack of broken bones. She broke the girl's arm and was trying to break her neck, pulling back on her hair with her knee stuck between her shoulder blades. I called for help. Two young nuns arrived but were useless. A hurricane was tearing through the room, habits gusted around like medieval capes. The beast continued to attack Analía. Father Ariel, the confessor, arrived and tried to undo the violent knot in which the two children were tied. He failed. The gardener came and knocked Chela on the head. She let the girl go and turned turn her attentions upon the man. They fought as equals. A half-dead Analía was smuggled out. A minute later Chela was acting as though nothing had happened. Analía was taken to the infirmary. I had a terrible headache.

"What can I do?" the Superior asked. "If news of this gets out, the parents will remove their children."

It was decided that I should take on the burden of going to the estate to ask them to come and pick up Chela immediately.

Mr. Stradolini, dismissing the severity of the incident, said that he'd go as soon as he could.

They locked Chela in a punishment room containing a coffin with a skeleton. Chela forced open the door and burst out like a furious beast. Instead of attacking, she recited verses

by Rimbaud in her man's voice, the one I'd
heard in the attic.

I am slave to my baptism.

Parents, you have caused my disgrace

and yours.

Poor innocents . . .

Priests, teachers, professors,

you are wrong to hand me to the

authorities.

I was never one of you,

I am of the race that sang from the

gallows.

I do not understand laws,

I lack moral feeling.

I am a brute;

you are wrong.

There was no one in the courtyard. I was
left alone. Father Ariel walked slowly toward
me. Did he not know that he was heading
toward an abyss from which he would never
return?

"My child, María Micaela."

"Fuck off back to your whore mother."

"Why would I want to go somewhere so horrible?"

The freak smiled at the priest, the priest took a case from his deep pocket and offered her a cigarette. She took it and they both sat down on the ground to smoke.

"I have a gift for you from your father," said Ariel.

He held out an envelope.

"As you can see, it's a pair of tickets to Europe. The other is for María Assuri."

"Please, ask my father to let me stay at the estate this summer."

We went back to the estate. Ariel moved in too. I had returned with them, but I was a wreck and determined to resign. I saw that Chela had grown, she was now a little woman of ten years old. That night, she would eat with the Stradolinis. In the dining room, on the large wall, a Venetian mirror reflected the entire scene: Chela was almost pretty in her pleated skirt and embroidered blouse, wearing white shoes with low heels. In time, she'd come to look like the elongated women painted by Modigliani. Lula was

eight and helped to lay the table. The mother,
newly pregnant, brought Juan Sebastián by
the hand. The father had aged noticeably, and
there was also Camelia, a friend of the household. Juan Sebastián was five years younger
than Chela and looked like a doll. An imbecilic dwarf, he mumbled "Mmm . . . mmm . . .
mmm . . ." in a repulsive manner, salivating
with hunger. Chela, who had just met him, must
have been reminded of her bout of rubella.

It was a silent dinner. Tense, I would say.
It was about to come to an end when Mr. Stradolini said something about the trip. I offered to
stay with Chela in the attic, considering post-
poning my resignation; I was very tempted by
the idea of going to Europe.

I tried to arouse her enthusiasm with a return to the pages of the *Revue des Deux Mondes*
and the article by Marcel Proust about Madame des Noailles.

We seemed on friendlier terms, so I said
to her,

"Do you still want to rub out the sky and
its burning sun with a giant eraser and paint 'la
champagne' in the pond with its rusty fish?"

"I shall never be a hirondelle d'argent," she replied wearily.

If I'd suspected what she was scheming, I would have followed her into the fields on the morning that she climbed onto the plow and set off, leaving cracked branches and a furrow of earth and stones in her wake. She flipped the harness and the plow fell on top of her. I heard an ominous crack similar to the one suffered by Analía. The victim was treated and given a pin and a cast whose profile echoed the harp in the corner. The trip was canceled.

At night, in the gloomy room we shared, I thought I could hear the owl's "Hoo . . . hoo . . . hoo . . ."

"I didn't kill Bertoldo, I just helped to save him from future sorrow and loneliness," she said.

I pretended not to understand, as though I were half-asleep.

"What's that, Chela?"

There followed a slow, fearful silence because the objects in the attic were under the influence of a spiritual energy I did not comprehend. Everything in the room began to move. The harp played faintly on its own, as though the strings were being plucked by a speck of gold, and the Manila shawl that covered her dropped to the ground like a dead peasant.

Perhaps I'd had a glass too much wine, perhaps it was the eerie atmosphere of the attic that persuaded me to interpret the "Mmm . . . mmm . . . mmm . . ." as the song of summer. But suddenly I saw the dwarf boy, who had climbed the staircase and now jumped onto my bed and started to snap his jaws. Chela banged her brace against the wall and the plaster came away from her arm.

That was why I left. Why I abandoned my mission long before it was completed. Because I am a woman of science and not an exorcist.

The Competition

Half a century later, I reread the pages that María Assuri called a "Report." So many mistakes, such ignorance of the psyche, its lights, shadows, and everything else. María was not a psychologist, she was a "lecturer in elementary psychology," a half-educated teacher.

In the same chest I found faded remains with heavenly flourishes, and although María Assuri was unfair, all the dried pages and cards with bunches of violets sweetened my mood without undue sentimentality. I don't believe that I hit Analía that hard; all I can remember of the event was rolling around on the floor, a struggle and the crack. I shan't take the trouble to analyze the aforementioned report.

Juan Sebastián came up to the attic, he had decided to live

there. He chose me and I accepted him; as a pair of freaks, we adopted each other.

"I shall teach you to think, I shall teach you to speak."

"Mmm . . . Mmm . . . Mmm . . ."

He understood.

Sara brought down María's bed and carried up Juan Sebastián's cot; that gave us more room. I ordered some books for my high school studies and to prepare for my university entrance examination.

I would repeat "Che . . . la" to my little brother. I wanted someone I loved to say my name.

Juan Sebastián observed my lips as closely as a dog eager to please its master. I kept going, "Che . . . la."

Finding it difficult, or perhaps impossible, to do what he was asked, he hid away in shame.

My love for Rimbaud continued, as either catharsis or resignation, and of course I read to Juan Sebastián too. He listened adoringly.

> *Perfect unforeseen beings*
> *shall offer themselves to your experiments . . .*
> *Magical flowers shall hum,*
> *sheltered by the slopes,*
> *geniuses of an ineffable,*
> *unconscionable beauty.*

He lurked in the gloomy shadows, "Yes . . . yes . . . Che . . . la."

My brother clapped because the brilliant rhythm of the verse, one of the few truly written verses the world has ever seen, struck some untouched chord, and the voice and words flowed forth.

Words and voice had been conjured by the sinuous, sublime pentagram of a strange poem by one of the purest poets who ever existed.

"Yes . . . Yes . . . Che . . . la."

My drooling little brother, an accursed creature, was applauding the light, the essence of beauty, perfection, from across an unfordable chasm. He showed off his two words leaping like a cat around the attic, doing cartwheels like a court jester.

His copiously flowing saliva began to leave trails from the bed to the bookshelf.

I gave him an occupation: to pick up balls of paper I threw to the floor and put them in the wastepaper basket. He embraced the task and began to resemble an old, dutiful trash collector determined to do his job well. In a way, Juan Sebastián was a talisman who lifted my spirits for a while. Every newspaper and magazine that Sara slipped under the door was picked up by my brother's little hands and passed to me with some effort. One of the newspapers brought an advertisement for a literary competition for young authors. The article was entitled "Ediciones

Roux Competition for Young and New Writers." The prize was publication of the work.

To be polite, I suggested to my little brother that we write a short novel together and he agreed with his two words. When I had finished, I read it to him and he approved, "Yes . . . Yes . . . Che . . . la." I went to the post office and mailed it in.

What María says about Father Ariel is true. He still lives at the house. In the now remote era of Juan Sebastián he would watch us climb trees and chase insects, catching guitarrero beetles with their lovely electric-blue shimmer, skinny as medieval jesters, and making them sing trapped in our hands before releasing them into the vivid skies of the Buenos Aires summer. He would watch us steal meat from the fire at roadside stands, to be naughty but also out of hunger because by now we were utterly neglected.

"Il testone ostinato," said the Italian hands, "El cabezudo," said the Spanish ones. My brother looked more terrifying year on year. And he was. The dragonflies and fruit passed on, the green faded. My little brother, part insect, part fruit, part flower, would be just as ephemeral. And of that blissful life of gnomes and spirits there would remain only a murmur, a hum, a fragrance, a drowsy sensation. We lived in our shabby garret, crawling around like lizards without a sound, following the scent of food, climbing into the fowl trough, or trundling along with the herd of cows to the water tank. However, there was some commotion when the Mozart and Beethoven records were found to have been scratched by barbed wire and Juan Sebastián pronounced his two words. When he slept, he purred like a cat and I studied for my final examinations. Meanwhile, I stared at his dirty nightshirt, his tiny Lilliputian feet, and the enormous empty head on the pillow. But I knew that his horrifying appearance concealed a beautiful soul.

Our unique form of orphanhood combined with the horrors of the night to create a desert, a lament, a blind zone.

And so we compensated: I, who never needed anything from anyone; he, who needed everyone but only had me, to tend to his rashes, bumps, bruises, fevers, and the night terrors that tossed him out of his cot like a sparrow from its nest during a storm.

Sometimes I would wake him up, shaking him, afraid that he had died, his breathing was so shallow. A poem by Rimbaud helped me to put together the puzzle of our lives; on their own each piece meant nothing but when the concave and convex edges were slotted in place they made a whole:

> My sad heart leaks at the prow,
> My heart covered in garbage.
> Splashes of soup pour over it.
> My sad heart leaks at the prow.

It had been weeks since Sara last came up to clean, and although my brother worked hard picking up the balls of paper, our filth-strewn floor disgusted us, albeit not so much as the polished, carpeted floors of the people house.

One day, Sara came with news.

"Your parents are going to France with the tickets you didn't use. Lulita will become a novice with the Carmelite nuns and, as Miss María has left, I shall take charge of Juan Sebastián."

"We'll see . . ."

Juan Sebastián, clinging to my discolored pants, babbled his two words urgently.

"I'll take charge of the boy," Sara repeated.

"Why can't you leave us alone?" I shouted.

The maid realized that she was in some danger.

When our parents left, we took possession of the house. We invaded the kitchen and the cook fled, we grabbed the salami hanging from hooks and bit off the ends, chewing on the flesh. We played football with the round cheeses. We ate like we never had before. The cook cried in the little courtyard and Juan Sebastián wiped his snot on her apron, then forced her into the pantry and hit her. My brother slid across the counter, from one end to the other with the poise of a skier, and I followed suit.

We took our revenge on the place where they kept the food.

Now the absolute owners of the people house, we howled

in the night like wolves and rolled around in Lula's pretty bedroom, on the white blanket, the pillow embroidered with her
initials, on the blue carpet.

"Are you sleeping here?" Sara asked in horror.

"One night here, the other there . . ."

"You'll drive me away from here."

She cried like a little girl. Then she locked herself in her
room, we heard the click of the lamp and the clack of knitting
needles. I savored some fourth-year theorems while my brother
jumped on the soft mattress like a jack-in-the-box. I studied
theorems, and my brother kept on jumping.

"Let's give Sara a scare," I suggested.

He clapped. We went down the hall and out into the garden. The mosquitoes tormented us . . . The house's windows
were, and still are, thick and tinted like stained glass. We could
see the maid through one of them in her white nightdress and
bonnet. She'd stopped knitting, now she was reading her prayer
book, flapping her fat mouth, exorcising demons. She turned
off the electric light and lit the silver lamp, from whose spout
danced, then and now, nymphs and fauns. The attic creatures
plotted mischief while the mosquitoes devoured our legs. Suddenly, she sensed us looking at her: she turned toward us and
crossed herself.

"Bring the horn," I said to my brother.

The gnome scampered inside and brought back the phonograph horn through which I recited some verses from *Maldoror* that I knew by heart mixed with some of my own invention that made them more relevant and scarier:

> *Oh, silver bucchero lamp,*
> *my eyes make you out in the dark,*
> *comrade from the cathedral vaults,*
> *my eyes wonder why you cast light*
> *on that dirty maid.*
> *Are you perhaps forced*
> *To serve trash?*

I was accompanied by the boy's howls. His eyes gleamed like Bertoldo's. I went on:

> *I had in my hand*
> *the rotten trunk*
> *of a dead man*
> *and I brought it from*
> *my eyes to my nose*
> *from my nose to my mouth.*
> *That is what Sara eats,*
> *flesh from the grave.*

She didn't dare close the chestnut shutters, she was frozen in place like a rag doll, an Astrakhan lamb awaiting slaughter. Her hysterical squeal annoyed us. I sang in the deep, hollow voice of a caveman:

> *We shall slip through*
> *the slats,*
> *we shall slice you into pieces*
> *and we shall dev-our you.*

Juan Sebastián pressed his ugly face against the glass and the maid fainted onto her straw mat. We went back up to the attic. I read about math until four in the morning. My little brother slept. The golden angel plucked her harp. I covered my brother with the Manila shawl.

The next morning, the mailman brought happy news: the envelope read "Ediciones Pastor Roux" and was addressed to Miss María Micaela Stradolini.

"They've asked me to come on Tuesday, and today is Monday," I said to Juan Sebastián.

"Yes . . . Yes . . . Che . . . la."

I found the publisher's address on a map of Buenos Aires. I looked for something to wear in the wardrobe and found a light blue dress with pleats and pearls. I cleaned the white shoes with the low heels and dried them on the duvet. I showered, brushed my hair, and poured an entire bottle of scented water over my-self. At seven in the morning, dressed already, I put forty pesos I took from a drawer of my father's desk into a leather purse and walked to the station, where I bought a ticket to Buenos Aires.

I felt a little dizzy. The nerves . . .

Some boys called out, "Hey, baby."

I was about twelve years old but was tall for my age. Some of our neighbors were in the same carriage.

"It's the eldest Stradolini girl."

I knew them, the Mendizábal spinsters.

"Is it three or four now?"

"Three. The lady lost the last one."

"I've always said that money doesn't bring happiness."

I listened harder.

"Hey, do you remember the grandfather? He lived in Paris."

"Where he got syphilis."

The old woman with the longest tongue went to the bath-room and I followed her. She took out dentures to rinse her mouth and left them to the side of the sink. I brushed the dis-gusting prosthetics with my purse and stamped on them when they fell to the floor. There was a crack of broken bones. The old woman gathered them up, sobbing.

"Look what you've done," she whined through her crum-pled mouth.

"I'm sorry, it was an accident."

I went into the cubicle to pee, pleased with myself. I had ruined their day out in the capital. They got out at a random station. I so wished my brother could be there with me.

I checked the location of the publisher on the map. Playing at being a free citizen, I browsed the shop windows and drank coffee. I smoked. I arrived at the publisher's at ten and was told to wait. I dozed off on a soft green leather chair.

"What do you want, girl?"

I met Roux. He was French and had a beard. I told him why I was there. I saw that he was surprised by my age.

"Did your parents bring you?"

I told him that they were away, traveling.

"Have you had lunch?"

He invited me to lunch and while I ate, he drank cognac.

"Do I seem very young to you?"

"I didn't think you would be so young."

"The competition didn't have an age limit."

"You've won it."

We went back to the publisher's and he sent for a printed copy of my novel, which had grown so skinny after being typeset that it looked like a brochure.

"So, you're a child, which means I need to talk to your parents."

He walked me back to Constitución train station, paid for

my ticket, and also bought me a silver box of chocolates and a bunch of roses. He didn't kiss me. I realized that he was afraid I'd fall for him.

I took the seven o'clock train, smoked a cigarette, and felt something, something incredible, like Greta Garbo. I had a bunch of roses, a box of candy, a package of books . . . my books . . . something that belonged to me. What a strange sensation.

My soul soared, it was sweet as honey candy. *This must be happiness*, I thought.

"Who's the chump?" some boys called out. Can so much change on a single trip?

Night fell, and I got back to the house. Juan Sebastián was waiting anxiously; I gave him the box of chocolates. He made the room sticky, getting chocolate on everything he touched. He undid my package of books (our books), piled them up, and said his two words. I knew he was happy too. I felt bad for leaving him alone for a few hours. It started to rain a "drizzle so fine that it doesn't seem as though it's raining," as López Merino put it. My brother danced like a little jester to the patter on the roof.

My parents returned from Europe in 1934. Meanwhile, I still had to pass the exams for three subjects before I could attend university. I continued my home schooling. I passed. Mr. Roux came for a visit and my father threw him out on his ear. They did the paperwork so that Father Ariel, now living on the estate, could be named what we called my "intellectual guardian." The little novel, which a long time later I would compare to *A Certain Smile* by Françoise Sagan, was my premature little daughter.

"Let us give thanks to the Lord," said Ariel.

We headed for the chapel. Father Ariel and Mr. Roux chatted about religious iconography, and when he saw the image of the saint urging silence with one finger to his lips and the other hand holding a staff, the good editor remembered his native Paris:

"It's Saint Marcel."

At the foot of the image writhed a dying dragon.

"Why is he hurting it?" I asked.

"It's an old story from Paris," Mr. Roux explained.

We didn't know it.

"Women are always the cause of wonderful and terrible things. A serpent was sleeping in its rightful place, among the stones of the walls of Notre Dame. Around that time, the Sinful Duchess passed away and was buried somewhere very close to the great serpent's nest. Always hungry, the reptile devoured the body of the duchess, whose soul it had taken when she was alive.

"As a human body has four limbs, there's no need to explain how a dragon was formed, and it ravaged the city for many years. Then Saint Marcel opened the crypt and killed the monster with his staff. He was always silent about the horrible event, a fact commemorated by the finger to his lips."

"A few of us thought that it referred to the secret of confession," said Ariel.

"The church has a few secrets," Roux replied.

Miraculously, this was the beginning of a good period for me. I wrote for several magazines, and *El Día* and *El Argentino* newspapers in La Plata. My father suffered from angina in his chest. When he summoned me to his study, I felt panic again.

"You are more emboldened and arrogant than ever. When has there ever been a similar case, a noted intellectual who eats from the same bucket she defecates into?"

I was amused by the word *defecate* in my father's mouth, surrounded by the mustache and beard, behind which a red lip pressed against the upper teeth to pronounce the "f." I almost burst into scandalous laughter. I grew brave.

"Father, you can't touch me because you are already dead."

The old man trembled. I fled, peeing myself on the spiral staircase up to the attic. I could barely breathe, my panic was so brutal. My father died five days after hearing my voice for the first and last time.

"Don't come to the wake with your brother, come alone," said Sara.

I went to see my brother.

"Father died."

"Yes . . . yes . . . Che . . . la."

He came down with me to the people house. "Mmm . . . Mmm . . . Mmm . . ." He wept over his father. Suddenly, he raised his big head and looked at me, seeing that I wasn't upset. Then he leaped about and did cartwheels, urinating on the foot of a chair. Sara tried to catch him and he spat at her. He bit a lady. Lula fainted and some nuns ran to her aid. I caught Juan Sebastián and during the struggle the sorry creature released something more solid than piss.

How we laughed up in the attic listening to the murmuring of prayers for my father's putative soul.

Mr. Roux came in his new car and, just for the ride, we went to the cemetery.

We were preceded by a caravan of horse-drawn carriages, also a few cars, and at the front of the procession, proud, imposing, and solitary as ever, went my father stretched out in his black coffin, in a hearse drawn by four black horses like the ones that transported the famous visitor to Dracula's castle. When we came to the desolate plains, I remembered some verses by Rimbaud:

> One takes the red path
> to get to the empty inn.
> The castle is for sale;
> its shutters closed.

Around the moors
the houses of the keepers
are uninhabited.
The fences are so high
that only the brooding peaks can be seen.
Has the priest taken the keys to the church?
But there's nothing to see inside.

The caretaker and the priest opened the Stradolini de Caserta Salina pantheon. Dark lees had begun to gather in the veins of the Etruscan marble.

The Apartment

I passed the three exams I had left. I had just turned seventeen when I enrolled at the Faculty of Humanities and Education Sciences. I signed up for the degree in philosophy and searched for an apartment so I wouldn't have to travel, choosing one close to the woods. I would share it with Clarisa Vieytes, a "chronic" student who was already living there.

I was stricken to be parted from Juan Sebastián. Sara would take care of him because my mother, now free, had decided to resume her musical studies at the Faculty of Fine Art.

To get away from Clarisa, who came to my room far too often, I took a course in typing and shorthand. I would take notes in classes and sell them at the Student Center to make myself independent from the allowance given to me by my mother.

I took my exams in November, December, and March: I wanted to get my degree as soon as possible so I could study for my doctorate. In November, I passed seven courses with distinction and my fellow students became my former fellow students. I was exiling myself again. I could see that.

I never went to a party or a dance. When it came to the cinema, I went when I was sure that the film would be worthwhile. By the December and March exams, I was already regarded as a "freak."

I met Carlitos Ringuelet, an excellent student and poet with whom I could speak French. I think that, if I had had the time, I would have fallen in love with him because I felt something different when I was with this already quite mature and elegant beau, but he was married and things didn't get very far.

One rather Byzantine La Plata afternoon in December, when the air was thick with linden blossoms and magnolias and the Christmas pines and pastries were out, Carlitos Ringuelet said to me, "Your eyes have been across the Mediterranean."

I looked at myself in the mirror and was not unpleased.

"Why do you study so much?" he asked.

"It's easy."

He was a brilliant "chronic" who intentionally failed some of his exams because he needed the air of the cloisters, to walk the courtyards and corridors of the building that meant life to him in this life.

Clarisa never missed an opportunity to come into my room. An inveterate "slacker," she had failed her other courses and took philosophy so as not to have to return to her hometown.

"Why do you keep at it if you don't like to study?"

"I don't want to go back home."

I prudently asked no further questions. She threw herself down onto my bed and smoked at length. Pouting and vulnerable, she tried to make me talk.

"Do you have anything to drink?"

"Orangeade."

"Come to my room, I have everything."

She had everything except for books. She poured two whiskies.

"Clarisa, I don't drink."

"Don't worry, they're for me."

Clarisa was twenty-two. I told her that I was going to switch from Latin and Greek to anthropology.

"I don't care, I'll go with you. After all, I started with medicine and it didn't go well, then law and it went awfully, and now I'm shit at philosophy," she replied.

I looked at her more closely and shivered. She was an enormous magnolia, a giant, brazen flower. She had something of the still life about her, something rotten. In truth, the only thing about her that was alive was her cold but dormant hair, like a tangle of seaweed that wrapped itself around things: the doorhandle, the typewriter, a stylograph, the button on some-one else's blouse. Her hair preceded and followed her like the wings of a strange bird. I was afraid to get too close to Clarisa in case a gust of her silk caught and drowned me in its dark, wet currents. I tied my hair up in a ponytail.

"Let it loose," she said, pulling on the ribbon.

I saw the difference and realized that at the very least I needed to trim my split ends.

Clarisa seemed to read my mind.

"I'm going to give you a trim."

She took out some oil and a pair of scissors and, while she set to work, asked,

"What are you doing tonight?"

"Revising."

"Are you crazy? Let's go to the movies."

I went back to my room, revised and studied until two in the morning. Clarisa knocked on my door.

"I was wandering around, got bored, and came to study with you."

She was acting strangely, she seemed quite disoriented.

"Are you going to take Introduction?" I asked.

She tried to distract me.

"Hey, what's that?"

"A Chinese vase, can't you see? Don't waste my time, pay attention or leave," I added irritably.

She left like a bird with a lame wing.

I was able to avoid her for a week. I saw her in the Introduction to Philosophy class, smiling stupidly from her desk. I was always able to find an excuse to give her the slip.

I tried to speak to Professor Coriolano Alberini, but he always hobbled away from me on his crutches. I felt bad when that happened. Maybe, on another level, that was how Clarisa felt?

I passed three exams with distinction.

Clarisa smiled and failed, she wasn't a wounded bird anymore, she was a dying one.

She caught up with me on Calle 47 and begged me to help her prepare for psychology. I did and she passed.

She was bursting with joy and I felt sorry for her. The idiot seemed to touch something inside me.

"I could never understand psychology but you made everything clear for me."

She grabbed my head and kissed me on the lips. Confused by the smell of tobacco and scotch, I felt very embarrassed. She continuously invited me to the movies and to dinner and also decided to study aesthetics with me. I think that for a few hours she was sure she had tamed me.

I agreed to the aesthetics. Professor Guerrero was an implacable obstacle to mediocre students and aesthetics was tough.

Clarisa would never be able to handle the challenge of interpreting texts such as *Laocoön* by Gotthold Ephraim Lessing, but I would try different ways of stimulating a response.

"Listen," I said. "'Laocoön suffers like Philoctetes in Sophocles.' It means that Greek serenity is the opposite of tears and cries of pain."

When I got no answer in words and her expression didn't change, I performed some Greek theater: miming tranquility at first and then rubbing ash into my hair. Clarisa was silent.

"Only the Greeks stay dignified, and when they suffer, they do not cry out, while the Trojans curse and howl, they are the seed of savagery."

She started to weep.

"I'm sorry, you made me emotional."

"Silly, trite little girl."

In the *Iliad*, I showed her the plate of poor Laocoön and his unfortunate children.

"We shall work on different degrees of passion."

She didn't pay attention or comprehend anything. She smoked. I imagined her lit in the glow of a fir log fire.

I thought, *If only I can revive her, make her crackle like Meleager, see the flame burning her insides, melt this wax doll, prune this withering branch, which is already coming away, pluck this rotting fruit.*

"Do you think poetry came before sculpture?"

She answered as though returning from the lilac-blue shadows of the dead:

"Yes . . . Yes . . . Che . . . la . . ."

I hid my dismay.

"Clarisa, you're going to have to study on your own."

"Mmm . . . Mmm . . . Mmm . . ." she whispered.

Who had entered my room to put words and whispers known only to me in this tiny mouth?

I read a few verses from *Laocoön*:

> *Exposed to the inclemency*
> *of a turbulent sky,*
> *he lies there abandoned*
> *bereft of hope.*
> *Not a single friend, no one to*
> *accompany him in his misfortune.*
> *No one to calm*
> *his pain and share*
> *his tragedy.*

The silly girl resurfaced.

"Chela, I'm going to give you makeup so you can be pretty . . . You don't understand me . . ."

When she began to sob like Laocoön's two children together, I almost hit her.

"No one understands me," she hiccuped, dragging herself across the floor.

This mollified me, because no one understood me either. And that emboldened her. I felt something begin to creep between my legs. Oh, yes, it was Clarisa's hand. I understood.

I gave her a kick to the chin and with renewed and enhanced animal fury threw her out into the courtyard.

"Yes . . . Yes . . . Che . . . la," she whined.

"Tomorrow, I'm going back to the house," I said to myself.

Revelation

I returned to the house. I was wearing a cream suit, red silk blouse, low heels, and had cut my hair *à la garçon*. I sensed people looking at me. I enjoyed the view of the landscape as the sun burned off the mist; crystal tears glittered on the roofs. As always, I went in via the servants' entrance and climbed the spiral staircase to the attic.

"Juan Sebastián," I shouted.

"Yes . . . Yes . . . Yes . . . Che . . . la," he called back.

He leaped onto my neck with the howl of a dog lost and found. He'd turned ten but hadn't grown an inch. I unwrapped packages of gifts: little glass eyes, a red ball, chocolates and candy. He offered me the first candy and shoved two in his mouth at once. He was very skinny and very dirty. When Sara came in, he spat at her through the two pieces of candy.

"You're back, miss."

"So it would seem."

"I shall let madam know."

I heard my mother's piano, was she studying or practicing? What was that, Bach or just an exercise? Terrible. The two freaks headed out into the countryside. Running away, we ended up at the old red patio. Juan Sebastián had insisted on taking me there, as though he wanted to show me something. He removed the tile where we'd made our discovery, shoved his arm into the hole up to the elbow, and disinterred another dwarf. He'd found it himself and hidden it again until I came back. In our lonely legacy we were a pair of dead souls wandering the Etruscan family pantheon. Juan Sebastián touched the doll's oversized head and then his own: he'd seen an ugly similarity. We were a pair of spirits trapped inside our own tomb, or perhaps innocents who bore the burden of someone else's guilt? I would find out.

"Hellooo . . . Nutjobs," came the call, accompanied by the sound of galloping hooves.

"The nutjob's your whore of a mother," I answered.

Arnaldo, my cousin people now called Don Arnaldo.

"Why insult us, you bastard?"

"Hello, degenerates. What have you got in your hand there?"

He took the sculpture from my little brother.

"Let's play keep away."

He rode around us on his horse and we jumped like idiots trying to get the object back. Juan Sebastián was sobbing in despair, I threw a rock at my cousin and he wrapped his crop around my arm. My brother was coughing and panting. I picked him up and followed the nag's trail, which ended at the main entrance. The animal was tied to a post.

My mother was sitting at the piano and didn't turn around.

"How are you, Chela?" She went on playing in the same pose. "Mr. Roux has been telling me wonderful things about you."

Widowhood became my mother. She was looking very beautiful. My abominable grandmother was there, her orthopedic shoes poking out from underneath the black skirt.

"Do you know that your mother is going to give a concert?"

I let out my old cackle.

"Don't be an imbecile, why are you laughing?"

My little brother hopped around like a court jester.

"They're a pair of freaks," declared Arnaldo.

He put our discovery on the piano.

"That's ours, we found it at the old Angelina house."

"Morons . . . what do these morons get up to?"

"I'll kill you one day," I swore.

Juan Sebastián pounced on the figurine.

"Oh, María Salomé . . . our peace has been shattered, God willing your second marriage will be happier than the first," sighed the abominable grandmother.

At forty years old, my mother was courting. I felt sorry for her. To cut through the sentimentality in the air, I amused myself by taking my cousin's crop and lashing him until my hand, arm, and even my elbow had grown numb.

"His skin . . ." wailed the grandmother.

"Fairy, I hear the old pig smothers you in Parisian creams."

"Tragedy has returned to this household," Mother whimpered.

We fled to the attic. Juan Sebastián fell asleep, worn out by the battle in the people house.

"The French gentleman visits your mother and drinks tea with her, your grandmother, Mr. Arnaldo, and Miss Camelia."

A question came to mind. I didn't say anything. I heard the piano. My mother was playing whatever composer this was like a beginner. The grand hall was full of adolescent emotions. The scales were interrupted by the sound of two people laughing.

I went down to spy, as was my wont.

The grand hall was lit by Florentine candelabra and the grown-ups were playing in the darkest corners. Mr. Roux bestrode the room, a lusty colossus. He pursued my mother like an eager teenager, she lost a shoe and they rolled around on the carpet, engaged in amorous flirtation without progressing much further. I remembered my father and had to choke back a fit of laughter when I realized that it was I who had inadvertently introduced him to the man who would cuckold him.

"You shan't miss my concert."

"No, I'll be there."

This unleashed a stream of bearded kisses to my mother's neck. How disgusting.

"Stop it, that tickles."

"Yes, it does . . ."

I had to rush back up the stairs to keep from vomiting. Sara brought us up a tray with some food.

"Were you downstairs a moment ago, miss?"

"Yes."

I lit a cigarette and waited. She was nervous, but she'd ask her question.

"Did you see anything?"

"Do you mean whether I saw the geriatrics?"

She didn't understand and left. We took the tray and threw it upward, it spattered the ceiling and crashed to the floor. We rolled around in the liquid and oils just like mother and Roux on the rug of the grand hall.

Juan Sebastián threw custard at the door and some of the dessert spattered the face of Mr. Roux, who had decided to venture upstairs.

"Chela, I must share some very personal news that brings me great joy and I hope you will feel the same way."

"I know already."

In his confusion he was like a punctured balloon. My former affection for him had disappeared. I decided that I would try to give him a scare, if possible.

"Mr. Roux, do you see something like a ghost over by the harp?"

"No, nothing."

"It's a woman, the soul of Madelaine Fornier, she's just told me her name, 'Madelaine Fornier.'"

"Chela, you must be joking. My late wife's name was Madelaine Fornier."

One mustn't joke about certain things. A stiff, silken shape floated over toward Mr. Roux. My brother said his two words, but this time with devotion. The shawl fell when the harp strings hummed.

"Forgive me, Madelaine," sobbed Mr. Roux, who had fallen to his knees. He fled through the servants' entrance and never came back.

At a stroke I had brought an end to my mother's second flush of youth, or possibly her only one.

The Breed

I went back to La Plata to pay my university fees. Passing by a pet store, I bought a tortoise and made a hole in its shell through which I looped a silver chain. I gave it to Juan Sebastián and we called her Bertha.

My anthropology classes began. I climbed the stone staircase between the two saber-toothed tigers and behind the bust of Perito Moreno I found a mural of prehistoric images. At first, I didn't understand why verses by Rimbaud rang out in my soul:

> *Magical flowers hum.*
> *Sheltered by the slopes.*
> *Animals of wonderful elegance*
> *roam.*

Later, I realized why they had come to me: the poet must have belonged to a time before Time. I spent a long while there, reaching deep into the mural with a mental hand and arm, right up to the elbow. The limb was just as real as the one with which I had found the figurines. Then came my first class with Professor Cristofredo Jacob in the amphitheater.

The professor carried around a small stool because he liked to sit but also to be constantly on the move. In truth, he was a sedentary walker. The subject was the Ages of Prehistory. The teaching materials were slides projected onto a screen with a pointer.

I entertained myself looking at the claws of the Saurians, which were very well drawn, and the professor's hand, which was missing three fingers. He cut them off himself when he was injured by a bone doing research in Patagonia. For fear of getting gangrene. Prehistoric scenes were projected onto the screen. Later on, skulls filed by. First came the sorry-looking Pithecanthropus. Next the dynamic Neanderthal. Third, grandfather Cro-Magnon. And the windows of the amphitheater at the Museum of La Plata were a combination of blue-green and lilac. Aromas from the woods of La Plata filtered through the gaps in the old frames and the lead linings installed by the founders, which were almost liquid in texture. They were images by Ingres. Jacob encouraged us to dig into a putative, fragile, monstrous past.

Jacob's circle was difficult to get into and only the most capable lasted for any amount of time. He liked me and invited me to his office.

The papers in the attic include evidence of my scholarship, which spanned classes at the museum, the Faculty of Humanities, and trips to the estate. It was the best time of my life, most of all because when I knocked on the professor's door, which was located in the museum building itself, a garret where orderly chaos or vice versa reigned, I was welcomed by the wise, solitary man who counted me among his personally chosen entourage. Books and more books, papers and more papers, bones and stones, photographs, films, and the odd flower stuck in a clear vase of water. When he told me about his accident in Patagonia, he added "Girl" (he always called his favorite disciples "girl" or "boy"), "one must always act in accordance with the requirements of the situation, or your very survival will be at stake."

One very special afternoon, I told him that I would have liked to have had him as a father.

"You don't need one, you're naturally equipped to get by on your own. But you must stand on solid ground, otherwise the slightest ill-intentioned nudge will tip you over. Don't go looking for love, and if heartbreak approaches, don't let it topple you and throw you off course. Fight for yourself."

That afternoon, I wanted to ask him something, but he

continued rambling. "Everything has importance, even an insect, because it's full of vitality. Do you know who will die if they continue to act as nonsensically as they have up until now? Humans, who destroy everything that moves and consume the vitality of the universe until they themselves die of inertia when there's nothing left moving. You must respect life if you are to achieve complete self-sufficiency."

"Yes, yes . . ."

"What did you want to ask me about?"

"This."

I showed him the figurines. I was afraid he'd laugh me out of his office.

"Let's take a look at this trinket."

He scratched the surface of glass and terra-cotta with a knife.

"Girl, this is no trinket, it's a miniature copy of a cameo, or a late reproduction of a larger group. My God, these remind me of Doña Agustina Sarmiento and Doña Isabel de Velazco, this one looks like María Bártola and the children Nicolasito Petusato and Nicolás Hobson."

He then corrected himself.

"The girls look like María Bártola, because María Agustina and Isabel weren't ugly. Where did you get this?"

"From La Angelina."

"This is Italian and very old."

He gave me the address of a German antiques dealer.

"Can dwarfism be caused by *Spirochaeta pallida*?"

"It can."

"By inbreeding?"

"It can."

"By rubella?"

"It can."

The professor didn't know that I had a dwarf in the family, or about the rivers of incestuous blood in which I swam, or about the syphilis my grandfather caught in Paris. He didn't know about my rubella. Disregarding the fact that I could be a convert or the descendant of Sephardic Jews, he also raised his Aryan standard.

"For example, the Semitic people are going to die out due to repeated wear from sharing blood for centuries, generation after generation. Their individuals are now weak, deficient, degenerate. The syphilitic are rotten, and although treatment can sometimes be effective, I do not believe that a definitive cure is possible, they should be castrated."

He listed a series of cases. In the other matter, if the pregnant woman contracts rubella at three months, she should abort.

He spoke at length about events in Germany:

"We, the Aryans, shall go to the stars from which we came to fall on the steppes and spread across Europe. We shall return

to the sky like angels on chariots of fire because we have en-
dured suffering and amputated where necessary."

He held his hand between his eyes and the light.

"Mmm . . . Mmm . . . we shall travel in spaceships," he
whispered. The oil lamp exposed the stains on Jacob's old suit
and the thick hair on his head and face. His voice grew loud
and I was afraid it would wake the lizards from their long sleep.
"You'll see."

He said:

"I'll walk with you."

"Where do you live, professor?"

I was a very limber cat, he panted at my side.

"Where do you live, professor?" I asked again.

"In the catacombs, like the dead."

"Yes . . . yes . . ." (the influence of Juan Sebastián).

"Oh, you shall suffer greatly, girl. But don't change, and
don't seek happiness, there is none for people like us. Don't rot,
and don't get spattered by the rottenness of others."

We said goodbye at the edge of the woods where the as-
phalt begins. He disappeared among the branches of the tall
eucalyptus, heading for his attic.

The Cameo

I went to Buenos Aires to see the antiques dealer. His dinner consisted of torta negra cakes over the paper in which they'd been wrapped accompanied by coffee from a beautiful porcelain cup. He inspected the object at length. This all took place at the top of an extremely old Gothic tower.

"I don't eat much, this is my only meal of the day. Well, I'm an old man," he said apologetically.

Everything around him was old: the baseboards, the shelves, the walls, the objects, the mattress on which he slept.

"This is all perfect," I said.

"Look around while I study your find," he said.

He pointed to the zoetrope in the middle of the room, made in the shape of a cup and standing on a Mudejar base on the red velvet carpet. I went to the cup, spun the ring on its axis, and peeked through the symmetrical slats. On the other side danced animals of the jungle and forest, rivers and seas in a mysterious mist. It might have inspired Rimbaud when he wrote:

> *Far from the birds*
> *the flocks,*
> *the peasants.*
> *What did I drink*
> *on my knees*
> *in the heather*
> *surrounded by tender*
> *woods of hazelnuts,*
> *one misty, green*
> *and mysterious afternoon?*

"Are you thinking of Rimbaud?" asked the dealer.

"Can you read minds?"

"Your thoughts are my thoughts. All thoughts are shared."

He was an angular gentleman. His narrow, elegant body was bathed in light from a Murano lamp, bright in places and dark in others, wholly mysterious. I thought he looked like an eel with arms and legs. In his hand, my figurine opened a watery portal through which I would learn everything I so longed and feared to know. He sensed my anxiety and took pity on me.

"Why don't you have a look at my clocks and instruments? I'm also a watchmaker and musician."

He had soon completed his examination.

"My dear, I've found a date: 1848. There's an engraving of an Aeolian harp . . . The family was originally from Sicily. They weren't peasants or commoners: here, you can see the fleur-de-lis crest and a tiny stamp that reads, 'Constables of Caserta.'"

He consulted some incunabula and read, "The family lived in Sicily during the Bourbon period, when the Kingdom of the Two Sicilies was ruled by Alfonso Conde de Caserta." He pointed at the couple. "The gentleman is the Constable, the lady the Countess. The dwarves aren't jesters, they are the unfortunate offspring of the unlucky couple."

I didn't say a word, a great sadness had darkened my soul. The wise expert tried to soothe me with a harp. His homeland, Germany, played through the chords, the melody was distilled snow and ice and it fell on the Nuremberg glasses, the engraved lids of the pots, and the wooden medallions from the sixteenth century, filling a ceramic baptismal font to the brim.

The memory of my brother broke the spell and I left the tower. I interrupted my studies to care for him. He died a year later. He died on me but not before returning the two words I had given him. I buried my childhood and a large part of my adolescence with Juan Sebastián.

I was resolved to allow myself to live, just to live.

Thwarted Plans

I adopted Bertha and carried her around attached to her silver chain like a medallion. I rented an apartment close to the Faculty of Humanities and Bertha and I moved in.

I completed my university studies at the age of twenty. I wasn't planning on returning to the estate. I didn't want to teach class at a public school or the National College. I was offered a few hours at the Art College, but didn't take the job. I would try, as far as possible, not to become entangled in professional or emotional commitments, and not to make friends. I did translations from the French for a publisher and tutored home-schooled and failing pupils. My hopes of traveling to Europe having been thwarted by the war, I would go to Chile; my goal was to reach Easter Island.

But the devil had other ideas.

Mother got sick and sent for me. I arrived at the house shivering in my coltskin coat. The winter had covered the house in a blanket of frost, the ravaged trees looked like skeletal beggars, and a chick cheeped from somewhere in the eaves. My mother was a bundle of twigs thrown up onto the roof by a storm.

She was surrounded by my abominable grandmother, Arnaldo, and Camelia. Lula hadn't yet been summoned. Ariel prayed. She was dying and I felt nothing. The stove crackled away.

Someone took a bunch of wilted flowers from a vase. A presence only I could see took my mother, but we spoke first.

"Daughter."

How much better things would have been for both of us if she'd called me that before, long before.

"Daughter, Chela, I'm going."

For some reason, I replied,

"Yes . . . Yes . . . Che . . . la."

"I want to ask you something in private."

The others left the room.

"You must insist that my remains be cremated. I'm afraid of worms, they've always disgusted and horrified me. Every two years, I have renewed my membership to the Chacarita cemetery, everything is paid up and properly witnessed. Make sure that my wishes are followed."

Lula arrived during mother's wake. She made a face when I told her about our mother's final wish. I realized that it wouldn't be at all easy to carry it out. Although I was supported by Arnaldo and my grandmother, Lula and the group of nuns with her, after crossing themselves, threatened to go to the bishop, to the Vatican if necessary. My mother hadn't known that it takes only one member of the family to object to prevent a cremation. I would sue.

I would keep my word to the deceased and upset Lula in the process.

The days passed.

For the moment, my mother's coffin would rest in the chapel, not the family pantheon as Lula wanted. There were other coffins in the chapel. I wasn't present when they put Mother in the box. One afternoon I went there, but I didn't know which coffin was hers, they were all recently polished and in a good state of repair. Which was it? I was playing a morbid game of chess, what move should I make?

Bah. I was sick of it. I'd lose the case.

And just when I least suspected it, I received a telephone call from Lula.

Over the brief conversation, she suggested how we should divide up the property and arrange for sale of the land. She chose the best lots for herself—otherwise she'd go to court—and I would get the dry land where I could tend to my

succubi, incubi, and green gremlins. Ariel helped me with the
paperwork.

Back in the chapel, I asked Ariel,

"Which is my mother's coffin?"

"Chela . . . I'm not sure . . ."

The six coffins looked as though they were crowding
around a statue of a saint.

"This one maybe?"

"Perhaps."

Playing guessing games with the dead, that was all I needed
in my solitude.

"Is opening it the only way?"

"The only way."

Fifteen days after her death, I saw her again. Ariel and men
who had come to transport her to the Chacarita were there. I
remembered medieval prints of the Triumph of Death and a
hitherto unfelt tenderness toward my mother fleetingly brushed
over my skin. I didn't cry. I abandoned her to the purifying
flame. It was an unpleasant afternoon in August 1941.

And suddenly I was taken back to my four-year-old self,
the little girl dressed in organdy in the dark photography studio. On the sandy paths of the cemetery, I dipped my shoes
in the rain puddles. I heard "Freak" and knew that for me my
mother had died long before, one far-off day in 1925.

The Napkin

I felt an urge to have a strawberry ice cream so powerful that my stomach hurt and my throat dried up. I got back to La Plata in a terrible state. I took a taxi to the usual café.

Among my papers I keep two napkins stained strawberry red. In La Perla I sat in the same chair as before and ordered a strawberry ice cream; my bronchial lobes wheezed.

"Isn't it a little cold for ice cream?"

The man sat down in my mother's chair from that long-ago day. I knew that I was trapped and needed to unburden myself to someone. I told him about the sad scene I had just been involved in. He smiled, he was a doctor and had seen many similar and plenty that were worse. He drank port after trying my ice cream and using my napkin.

To lighten the mood, we discussed films and Charlie Chaplin. He loved "La Violetera" and asked the waiter whether they had it. I knew that they did. The syrupy music floated up and sweetened the atmosphere like an innocent, confused bee trying to drink from the decadent flowers on the baroque café ceiling. We introduced ourselves, we were both from La Plata.

He was already aware of my incipient literary career, the city was still small enough that one knew with whom they were speaking.

"It's a privilege to be sitting here with you."

I noted a hint of irony.

"My eldest son is your age."

I noted a hint of despair. And that this man would change my life forever.

I wanted to sob into his lapels. I controlled myself.

I should have cried like so many other people do, almost everyone. That way, I wouldn't be so alone and treasuring a single moment of clarity: September 21, 1941.

The reflected glow from the Río de la Plata, our only conversation in Luis's car. There was no other light. The spring sun was plunging downward and boys were playing football.

"The witching hour," Luis murmured.

Luis smoked. I clung to his side like the carapace on a crustacean. I was always a little slimy, a little clumsy sliding up and down his body, wet with tears and mucus, maybe, and now I know I must have put off the mature gentleman who opened my eyes and patiently bore the first flushes of my love. All I wanted to do was merge and become one with the body of this distant man. I was struck by a desperate need to possess him, I relinquished my reason, and it was a dangerous, cruel affair because I was stumbling across unfamiliar terrain, the scorched terrain of love.

I bit off a piece of his lapel and chewed on it.

"What are you doing, you crazy girl?"

He realized that I was going to swallow it.

I guzzled down the nectar of his company. It was a way to make him part of me. I bit his lips. I bit him all over. I was living in a newly emerged realm of love, a desperate tragedy, a pitiless orgasm for someone who had never even been kissed before. If I could have devoured him, I would have ingested his body into my guts and he would cease to be beholden to his obligations as a husband and father, government official, and society figure. I wouldn't leave a trace of my beloved for anyone else.

Not for anyone else.

And the sorry figure received caresses that had been pent up for twenty years, rough and cloven.

"You're a terrible little beast," he groaned.

Looking back, I know better. He was an ordinary man and I was his crazy lover. It was an uneven match. An impossible union. I trod his beloved expanse like a blind person reading braille, leaving nothing unuttered, looking for the springs, the veins, the tiniest pore that might release complete and inimitable ecstasy. I didn't want to be alone anymore, I didn't want to be the solitary creature from La Angelina, I would rather be a beast blinded by passion trying to regain my sight through the eyes of love.

"You're what I needed," he said.

In his long history of womanizing, he had never experienced anything like it. And, if he survived it, he never would again.

"I don't want to share you," I said.

"Where can you go, looking like that?"

I wasn't respectable. I lived in a street-level apartment. I was common. Sometimes it made me angry.

"Stay the night."

He couldn't. He was pulled this way and that by his people, his commitments, and meetings at the Jockey Club. He began to tidy himself in front of the mirror and I would mess him up again. I felt the cold from before, the familiar cold when he left because he was an ordinary citizen, a society man, one of many, and I couldn't understand why I loved him so fervently.

"Will you get a divorce?"

"Chela, we've been married for twenty-four years."

"I'm going to the country tomorrow."

He was afraid to lose me. I hit him where it hurt.

"Even if I never see you again, you will always be my great love."

He looked like a scolded teenager.

"Chela, I've never loved anyone the way I do you."

Grandmother had moved into the house. Arnaldo was playing at being a rancher. Sara looked like a diseased tree. Ariel had aged fairly well.

"Your cousin is engaged," Ariel told me.

"What isn't he engaged in?"

"He administers the estate and is courting Jacinto Gay's youngest daughter."

A girl rolling in money, the daughter of a Mendizábal.

The dentures of the woman from the train bit deep and malevolently.

"He'll help them to spend it at the racetrack," laughed Ariel.

The degenerate would bet on any two things you could race or pit against each other.

"When he marries, I hope he'll move out with the abominable grandmother."

"He wants to buy some land from you."

"He's smart."

That same day, in front of a public notary, I named Ariel my administrator.

To celebrate, that night we drank Lágrima de Cristo in the sacristy, toasting with lovely Murano glasses.

"You know, Ariel, I have a lover."

He choked on his drink.

"Why don't you get married, daughter?"

"Because he's already married, father."

"Daughter, God forgive me, but tell him to get a divorce."

"He's been married for twenty-four years."

"Leave the man, take pity on your soul."

"I'm in love, Ariel. Crazy to the bone."

"In love . . . What kind of a man must he be?"

"Like any other."

No, he couldn't be like any other. The empty house howled. Human and humanoid specters appeared in the windows. The carpets were covered by a dust in which a wandering spirit made prints with its deformed, muddy feet. Ariel looked very old.

"Marry a sturdy boy, someone well-educated, smart, or a rich Portuguese, and raise a herd of children at La Angelina."

"A herd of big-headed dwarves."

The priest tensed up, but a moment later we were both laughing uproariously.

"My dear little cousin . . ."

Arnaldo. I considered getting rid of him and the abominable grandmother.

"Hey, you could have warned me you were coming," he said, continuing the pretense.

"Why? So you could be ready with your nag to run me down?"

"You're a resentful woman."

The air of the sacristy filled with curses. Grandmother arrived with her bamboo cane. An ugly orthopedic shoe poked out from underneath her skirt. Sara came, looking dark and run-down.

The estate was a pantheon. I went out into the fields with Ariel. The sun shone brightly in the purple tufts of the thistles. Pollen bitter and sweet flew back and forth on the antennae of insects and a saintly aura inspired silence. Although we didn't speak, we were beset by similar melancholy thoughts. Dew ran down the windows of the greenhouses, as though the glass were crying. Ariel tested his inner devotion. I summoned my gremlins, Bertoldo and Juan Sebastián. We stood in the ruins of the original house. There was the patio with the red tiles and the hole where we had made our discovery.

After the land was divided, I owned the dry lots between the house and what had been La Angelina. My sister owned the land rented by the Portuguese, ideal for both crops and livestock.

I thought that my land was good for nostalgia and nothing more. We lit cigarettes in the ruins. I threw a rock into the south wind that swept over the barbed wire and masonry of the horrible place.

I heard: "Hoo . . . hoo . . . hoo . . ."

I heard: "Yes . . . Yes . . . Che . . . la."

We were in the last bastion of the estate, where my ghosts

awaited me. I sang an ancient lullaby in my hoarse voice and sunbeams made Goyaesque shapes as the barren fields yawned before us.

That night I went back to La Plata. Light filtered from beneath my apartment door. I remembered that Luis had a key. There he was, waiting for me like a teenager, feeding lettuce to Bertha, which I found both touching and amusing.

"I'd like to take you out to the movies, they're showing one with Greta Garbo," he said.

"Let me have a shower and we'll go."

Oh yes, Camille snapped like a sick reed. Sleet fell over Paris and also on my soul together with an unbearable anguish. Back at the café, which hadn't changed and nor would it, we made insignificant small talk to avoid more serious topics.

A popular song filled the naive Baroque hall, a stupid little song that got into my lungs, making me cough.

> *When you are truly in love,*
> *the way I love you,*
> *it's impossible, my dear,*
> *to live so far apart.*

Tears scorched my neck.

"I'm just a walking cliché," I said angrily.

"You're very young."

"Don't make me cry anymore."

"Let's go . . ."

In my apartment, we exhausted ourselves making love like a condemned couple.

"Will you get a divorce?" I asked.

"Wait a little longer, be patient." He sounded like a little boy. "I can't live without you, Chela."

"Does your wife know?"

"What isn't common knowledge in La Plata?"

"Why didn't you tell her yourself?"

He bit his right thumb, the same hand in which he held his cigarette, and told a story about how his wife was the governor's cousin and a potential promotion depended on the connection. He had to behave. A divorce right now would wipe away his aspirations like dust on a wet cloth.

I felt dirty. I needed a hot bath with plenty of soap. I thought of María Assuri, if she could have seen me like she had when I was a girl, she would marvel at how well, extensively, and thoroughly I soaped and rinsed myself. I kicked the door to the bathroom closed and got into the shower.

"When can I see you again?" he called.

"Tomorrow, I'll be having lunch in the usual place," I replied reluctantly.

I could sense it was better not to be seen with Luis.

In the restaurant, I found a table to the side with Bertha

in my pocket. I ordered a pork chop and lettuce. Meanwhile, I read Proust: "Nothing lasts, not even death."

I would smile when Luis arrived. I heard someone utter a greeting, "Good day, sir, how are you both?"

Shortly afterward, the soft hand of my beloved rested on my shoulder and I was horrified to hear the words "Let me introduce you to my wife."

I think I held out my hand as though through murky, unhealthy water. I was aghast to see Luis pull over a pair of chairs. He had decided that we'd have lunch together.

I have no idea what they said, I retreated either into my shell or Bertha's.

I have never been able to remember anything about the horrible meal whose purpose was to quiet the wagging tongues of La Plata society. I spent every minute thinking of ways to escape, but because I was now a socially adjusted person, I held out until dessert and walked the couple outside but did not accept their offer of a ride. I scurried away like a dog with a can tied to its tail. I closed up the apartment and went back to the country.

I decided that I would travel. I would go to Chile. So, in the middle of 1943, like a molar with a cavity filled torturously with boiling lead, aching throughout my skeleton, I crashed down upon the hard surface of Santiago.

I was sick with bronchitis and anxiety. I took sedatives and sleeping pills quite regularly but was confident that I wasn't an addict. I kept the "shots" in a little blue crystal bottle that I called my Aladdin's lamp and every time I opened it promised myself that this time would be the last. But the pain returned and I rubbed my lamp again.

The genie of serenity worked his magic, rising from the blue glass to drive away the terrifying ogres I had taken with me across the Andes.

Giddy in Chile

A Chilean poet who lived in La Plata, Alfonso Gómez Líbano, who published *Suicide in the Waters* and *Denizens of the Night* when he was studying at the Faculty of Humanities, recommended me to a newspaper in Santiago and, at a reading of a new book he was working on, he introduced me to Pablo Neruda's circle.

Inside you, Diego de Almagro,
beats a heart like a bell
drilling out a deep valley,
when the wind blows, the shape
of a lithe warrior recovered from a fever.

Alfonso read out his long poem.

"What's it called?" Neruda asked.

"'Settler Blood.'"

He stopped reading.

Now the shots weren't enough, I was swimming in lysergic acid, like many of the intellectuals in Santiago at the time. Not that they were required, but the drugs made the rough-hewn, dangerous Neftalí Reyes seem even greater as he recited his poems in a voice that echoed from behind a mask or papier-mâché head. The smoke and drinks rose from my stomach to my mouth and I asked myself, *After hearing that, what's the point in writing anymore?*

He threw a bone to the other poets, inviting us to read something. I never did because I could see that he could barely keep his playful indigenous spirit in check and was always ready to laugh at us. One afternoon, he turned his maw toward me.

"You're not reading anything?"

"No . . ." I said, almost wetting myself.

Every other day, I brought my pieces to the newspaper in Santiago and in one issue I published an article about Neruda. I avoided the group for a week, a little out of embarrassment, a little out of fear.

When the giant moved to Isla Negra, I went uninvited and joined the entourage. As though through water, I heard him say something about the article. I don't know what it was about it that had amused him, but he wasn't scornful. I almost fell in love with Pablo.

I stopped myself beforehand, because he could never have enough women. And I had been inoculated against love. I felt tenderly toward him knowing that I was living in the attic of a giant who dwelled on his childhood poverty, a tin shack showered with pebbles by the wind. Pebbles that made dents when the wind flew into a rage. The poet's habitual gesture of covering his ears with his hands as though to quiet an ancient howl pained me.

"Were you born in Temuco?" I asked.

"In Temuco. Lost dogs bark in the oceanic night, choruses of tadpoles sing from the water and the yearning of these creatures flows forth to clash with the great murmur of the wind. The night passes that way, swept from shore to shore by the disdainful wind like a ring of dark metals cast from the north toward the southern belltowers. The solitary dawn, rocked and moored like a boat in dock, sways until midday and the lonely blue-roofed afternoon appears across the town, a large white candle from a lost vessel.

"Through my windows, behind the green fruit trees, beyond the houses and the river, three peaks lean on the tranquil sky. Brown, yellow parallelograms of plowed fields, cart tracks, thickets, isolated trees, uniform waves of golden cereals roll up the slope, breaking at the peak. Rain emerges onto the landscape and falls, spreading across the sky. I see the large golden sunflowers bow their heads and on the horizon the hills are darkened by a pulsing veil. It rains on the town, the water dances from the suburbs of Coilaco to the wall of hills, the storm rushes across the rooftops, heads into the farms, onto the sports fields, by the river, among the weeds and the stones, the poor weather fills the meadows with the debris of sadness. Rain, friend to dreamers and the desperate, companion to the inactive and the sedentary, shake up and grind your butterflies of melancholy over the metals of the earth, run along the antennae and towers, crash against the houses and roofs, destroy the desire to act and nurture the solitude of those with their hands on their foreheads behind windows, who require your presence. I know your innumerable face, I recognize your voice, and I am your sentinel who wakes up at your call during the terrifying earthly storm and leaves sleep behind to gather your necklaces while you walk the roads and settlements, ring out like a bell and dampen the fruit of the night, flooding your rapid, senseless journeys. So you dance, holding yourself between the livid sky and earth like a great silver spindle spinning at the center of your transparent threads. Heavy drops like fruit hang from the branches, the smell of the earth, of damp honeysuckle. I open the gate, stepping on fallen plums, walk beneath wet green hooks. Suddenly the sky appears among them like the bottom of my blue mug, recently washed by the rain, held up by the branches and dangerously fragile. The dog keeps me company, covered in droplets like a vegetable. Walking through the bowed corn, small showers fall and the big sunflowers bend, suddenly turning their large rosettes to my chest. Then you abruptly appear, corralled by the falling water, running stealthily through the storm to meet the hills, spanning two golden rings that get lost in the town's puddles.

"There is an avenue of eucalyptus trees, puddles underneath them, full of their strong winter fragrance. The great pain, the misery of things, gathers as I walk. The solitude is great around me, the lights climb the windows and the trains wail in the distance before heading into the fields. There is a word that expresses the sadness of this hour. Seeking it, I walk underneath the gloomy eucalyptus trees and small stars begin to appear in the darkening puddles. That is how night falls upon the hills of Temuco."

And all that from inside a big papier-mâché head.

I decided to indulge myself in some personal poetic catharsis. I went to Alfonso Gómez Líbano's publisher with a package of verses. He accepted and published them. Oh . . . I couldn't cleanse myself of all the sadness I had lived. I couldn't because ghosts from home spattered every verse with their filthy, enigmatic blood. I grew bold. I asked Neruda for a recommendation to write about and take photographs of Easter Island. I had the letter half an hour later.

After three years in Santiago, I left again, with a good camera and a portable typewriter.

Easter Island

Three hundred miles from the Chilean coast, the ground around Rapa Nui is volcanic, elephant gray, like a skin stretched over Atacama Province, of which the island is part. A lilac-blue cloud rises up from the sea and one encounters a landscape where you wouldn't be surprised to see Goya's demented Colossus sprout suddenly like a mushroom from the marina. On the ancient soils, which were softer at the time, enormous feet left their prints as messages to accompany the monuments. Huge stone heads emerge from the sparse vegetation, apparently made by a strange, lost civilization. Are they the gods of an unknown religion?

"They sing at night," a local informed me.

I found that this was true. At night, the wind sings from the depressions of the fifteen-meter-high face. To whom are these songs dedicated? Perhaps an argonaut people hidden by the Pacific? Perhaps the inhabitants of other islands that have foundered like the galleons of a fantastical, impossible fleet?

One hears the voice of the silent, ancient Rapa Nui homeland. One greets the crater, Ranu Raraku. One becomes an apprentice to volcanoes, like the young Pablo Neruda, seeing the tongues of Aconcagua, the fire of Tronador. And as described in his *The Divided Rose*, at night they see the fire of Villarrica scorching livestock as forests burn.

They say that the islands were created by clay, mud, and semen carried on the wind. Melanesia and subsequently Polynesia were created that way. The fingers of the Lord of the Wind sculpted the first statue out of wet clay, and with childish, mischievous glee knocked it down immediately. Then he built a second statue, this time of salt, and with the fury of a jealous artisan the sea dissolved it. But the Lord of the Wind showed that he was more powerful than all the others by sculpting the Moai Silence out of granite to last forever. Its Being stares out with a stony gaze. He smells with his prow-like nose. He measures distance with the clarity of a rectangle. The Lord of the Wind liked to multiply his stone cyclops through loving marriage with the breezes of Oceania, and so the enormous heads with the long necks and weighty permanence were born.

An unsettling permanence. Like eternity.

I wrote resting my typewriter on a flat rock, sending my pieces to the continent and receiving a stipend every month. I took clear, very interesting photographs. In a way, I had regressed to my pastoral childhood because I had my tea outside and my habit of talking to myself grew worse. More pernicious still, I was an addict, though I didn't dare admit it. One lilac-blue night, a crumbling face, fallen and broken, its nose buried in the calcareous crust of the island, the most sunken of them all, the one striving to return to the lava in the oceanic confines of the belly of the world, sang to me: "One and Perfect Love."

I fell hard to the ground and kissed the limestone, saying my goodbyes before returning to my country.

Back Home

I returned to the estate in August 1948, when the golden hedges of broom and acacia burnished the landscape with their glow. I thought I could hear an enormous harp being plucked for me, the far-off notes scudding like the clouds of a winter that would soon be over.

I weaved around the hedges, I was in no hurry to return after five years away. Ariel saw me and came running over. He had grown fat and matronly. We shared all our news.

"Your grandmother died in June."

"Aha . . ."

"Arnaldo got married and divorced."

"Degenerate."

"I sent a telegram to Santiago about your grandmother."

"I wasn't in Santiago, but it doesn't matter, I wouldn't have come back."

"Luis was widowed two years after you left, but I didn't think it was a good idea to tell you."

"Why? I would have come back."

"You can look him up. He left his address pinned to the wall."

"It's been so long . . . do you think so?"

"You should see him as soon as possible."

He continued catching me up: there had been a revolution in 1943 and a popular uprising in 1945. I'd read the news in Santiago and wondered what might happen to Luis now that his conservative party had been overthrown. Lula had been sent to Spain to learn the dogma. I spent a year at the house without daring to make a move toward Luis.

I took down the pinned address naming the street where my beloved lived without reading it. I sensed that I needed to protect myself. I went to La Plata, to a travel agency. I renewed my passport to be ready for any eventualities. Europe was my goal. The city was blooming with the aggressive scent of linden blossom. Moved by the elfin sweetness of my fellow youths and my heightened sensitivity, I felt the old pain in my lungs. Might this malaise flowing through my eyes and nose like water be an allergy?

Or tears. The ghosts and gremlins of the estate never would have let me cry. I cried over Luis. Aladdin's lamp. I took a pill from its curved blue crystal home and, thus emboldened, dared to read the address on the piece of paper I had removed from the pin. I drank coffee. The world was mine.

Bertha hung from my neck on her silver chain.

"Bertha, the world belongs to us now, let's go find him."

I euphorically rang his doorbell. A housekeeper or porter told me that the doctor would be back at four. After she closed the door, I slipped a note under it: I shall wait for you today and tomorrow at the estate, any time.

And that very day at six in the evening, his scent flooded the house and rose up to the attic. Intoxicated, I chided myself for the self-imposed parenthesis and ran down from my exile into what had been the people house to renew the era of love, the one and perfect love.

Luis was a changed man . . .

He formally held out his hand, and never looked me in the eyes. We made small talk and a little while later he said good-bye. I listened to his car rumble away until it was nothing more than a whisper.

I had been embarrassed when my father said, "Your mother gave birth to a boy." I envied the dead: my parents, Juan Sebastián, my abominable grandmother . . . and I mumbled some verses by Rimbaud that suited this accursed moment very well:

> *Lightning from heaven*
> *brought the comedy to an end.*

Oh, yes, I needed to sever, cut, prune, and raise anchor. How right I had been to get my papers in order.

A Parisian Beginning

The journey was delayed by mechanical issues. I slept a little, thanks to the pills. My only luggage was my sailor's sack, the same one in which I'd collected my finds with Bertoldo and Juan Sebastián. I read verses by Rimbaud in a volume I always kept with me:

> *I envied the bliss of animals,*
> *the caterpillars that represent the sleep of limbo,*
> *the moles, the dream of eternity.*

It felt as though a bolt from heaven had destroyed my comedy and plunged me into the *merde*. Ariel put money in my name in a bank in Paris. I had some more in my sack, just in case. I flew for fifteen hours. I got out at the airport in Paris alone, with no relatives waiting for me, and remembered the day of my first communion.

"Enough self-pity, we'll find a place for ourselves," I said to Bertha.

We were in a taxi on our way to the neighborhood by the Sacré Coeur. The chauffeur directed us to a room to rent above a bakery. I had a small shower partitioned from the rest of the diminutive room by a faded cotton curtain. The water swirled down a wooden drain. There was a harp-shaped clothes hanger. *Attics at every turn*, I sighed.

A delicious smell rose from the bakery. I went down to get some lettuce for Bertha, whom I left in a soap dish on the nightstand, before heading out into the night.

I was a hungry beast, a grieving animal shivering from the cold, on the point of howling in pain.

I wandered through lilac-blue shadows punctuated by Gothic needles until I got to the neon lights. I took a taxi for a while. The patisseries accentuated my hunger. The perfumeries conjured the ghost of someone who used lotion and French extract. I went into a bar. Close to the fire, I comforted myself with fish, potatoes, and chestnuts. I drank cognac and yearned for company. I was so skinny that I was afraid I was invisible. Because I took up only a small corner of the table, the rest was occupied by three youths. My plea was heard. I'd enroll at the Institute of Psychology along with them.

After dinner, they invited me to take a gargoyle shower, an owl's baptism. It was raining. Then the rain cleared and Notre-Dame's monsters vomited rusty streams of water into the Seine. Lying back, we were blessed with a water spell that transformed us into children of the Parisian night. I was adopted by three siblings: Pauline, Solange, and Jean. The four of us were connoisseurs of the aromas of lofts and garrets, to which we climbed up long, narrow, twisting stairs, the kind of string music few can hear because it is played by transparent hands, fingers with golden rings, doors whose moldy locks are opened by keys wrought like jewels, and the loving symbiosis that can turn anyone into an ideal, unique, and perfect love.

We amused ourselves by acting as though we were from another time. We spread ashes at the foot of acacias. We anointed ourselves with mandrake juice. With castor and camphor oil. And in feasance to our shared photophobia we shut ourselves in old chests until we could stand it no longer. I began to suffer from photophobia in Paris, because I lived in the neon nights of electric lighting and gas and kerosene lamps.

I had detected these three extraordinarily gifted creatures across the ocean with my own unusual antennae. Or had they detected me and brought me to them? We soon stood out in our psychology class.

We won posts as assistant teachers and so I was no longer dependent on the money Ariel sent and didn't have to queue at the bank anymore.

It was a winter's night when Solange threw herself in the Seine. She was fished out burbling among the vomiting gargoyles that foamed up the river by the shore. She was pulled out of the water like a long fish trailing weeds that had almost kept her bound to the riverbed.

She was revived and we brought her back to the garret by the Sacré Coeur. We lit the stove and sat in the tower, talking as though nothing had happened. The police believed that it had been a simple accident. Solange asked her brother for mandrake juice and he poured out a living, sparkling, whispering liquid whose vocabulary I understood.

Solange came out with us, her vigor renewed. She could walk only four blocks. Stretched out on a velvet sofa, she seemed to melt and you worried that the next time you looked over at her nothing would be left but a damp stain. She had spent twenty-four years being held up by her siblings. The brilliant invertebrate could climb anywhere. She looked like Michèle Morgan in *Pastoral Symphony*.

Our regular bar was decorated with a mural of crustacean carapaces: musical cockroaches, grasshoppers, locusts, shrimps, all playing instruments such as the guitar, the violin, and the viola, crafted by a patient artisan. This was the backdrop to Solange's repose, she joined the mural as a pale eel.

"What did you give her to drink?" I asked.

"Mandrake."

Solange was playing with a strange terra-cotta pendant that hung from a silver chain. I saw three faces forming a triangle and that it rotated.

"Show Chela," said Jean.

In my hand it throbbed like an artery.

"We're druids," the three of them said in unison. They owned a castle on land that had once belonged to the Carnutes. The property dated back to prehistory. The mansion was first built in 1200. And so the three Flamel of Taliesen siblings assimilated my spirit to theirs. They invited me to their home. We traveled all night by train, planning to take a week's vacation. They were going to hold a rite of initiation for a boy named Lazare, and although I didn't ask into what they were initiating him I realized that they were members of one of the many sects active in Paris. One entered the castle across what had once been a drawbridge but was now fixed in place. The Castilian fortress seemed as though it were keeping watch over the surrounding countryside through its portholes and opened up to the outside world through windows flanked by round towers with ancient moldings and crenellations. The structure of the garden pavilion matched that of the chapel. The three-faced motif appeared again on the family crest.

On it, I read *Eure-Cher*, the names of two rivers.

I admired the medieval banquet hall with its long table, area for servants and cupbearers, and platform for minstrels. My three friends disappeared. I climbed a spiral staircase whose steps were worn by centuries of use up to the shield room with its leather horses and wax knights in heavy armor peering their Gallic eyes out through visors like grief-stricken tigers, cats, or rabbits. I admired locks of hair set among ribbons and corselets in display cases. Everything was labeled and dated. I counted seventy-four. I was in the best attic in the world. I had no idea that I would one day experience something even more extraordinary, although that would happen sometime later.

I went out into the woods and found another spiral staircase next to a wall that led to an ancient garret. I climbed up and pushed on the acacia door. It opened at my touch and I found my friends behind it.

I don't know whether they were addressing me or talking among themselves.

"Solange is pregnant," said Jean.

"You should have been more careful," Pauline scolded.

"We didn't want to be careful," Solange replied.

I drew some momentous conclusions.

"We'll talk to Grandmother," Jean decided.

What would the old woman be like? As abominable as mine? I realized that the family's roots were sunk in murky waters. I remembered the patio at La Angelina and the find. I remembered Juan Sebastián.

Fifteen youths were invited to be part of Lazare's Rite of Initiation, all of the purest blood, which is to say they were descendants of the sect's founders. It was a very exclusive membership. I shall name only Jules and Sabine de Saint Germain, who were siblings. Sabine's husband was a crippled black man named Remus de Tamise. We were friends for many years. The aromas from the banquet in honor of Lazare mingled with candle wax, because there was no electricity. The torches on the walls cast a veritable shadow theater. A steady flow of cold fish and fowl was served along with champagne. I saw that Lazare's parents were nervous.

Because I was naturally predisposed to marvels of all kinds, I tried to connect with the spiritualists of the group. I plucked on old strings that were already throbbing, sharpened my radar and communicated with Whoever in the parallel universe, which was as real as ours. The shadows transformed Solange into a long stalk whose lips wrapped around the columns. She was wearing a green silk habit. Her brothers led her into the pavilion and we went up to the garret, which had a sign that read "Caveau." The congregation sat on benches in accordance with their status. I had no status and sat next to Jules, who was laughing uproariously. Jean began to intone an alchemical litany:

> *When the stone is perfect for someone*
> *it changes them from bad to good,*
> *it makes them liberal, sweet, pious,*
> *it removes the root of all sin*
> *remaining, heretofore,*
> *content with the graces*
> *they have obtained*
> *after the procession.*

"A processionary is a caterpillar that gnaws on holm oaks, it can eat everything except for real oaks," Jules whispered in my ear.

> *We are like the Processionary*
> *we are the consistency of eyelids*
> *and we torment those who*
> *try to destroy us;*
> *we tear our epithelia*
> *and are born as moths*
> *to settle in*
> *our totemic oak forest.*

"The ones in front are moths already, we're just caterpillars."

As a caterpillar, I started to crawl around the engraved walls, which were finished in blue-green enamel. A two-headed angel protected a young oak, a bird plucked feathers from its belly, three snakes poked their tongues out at the bird. Behind the angel was a lion with eight legs, two violin-playing goats, and a large black seal with the motto: *Spiritus Facro Fancti Gratia. Non Ex Mes Fcienti, Fed Ex.* From top to bottom of a thick column ran a list of symbols. I remembered a book from my grandfather's library whose copper covers protected sheaves of tree bark divided into three sections of seven pages each. The bookplate had the image of a snake wrapped around a staff and a second nailed to a cross while more Ophidia crawled out of a fountain. A caption adorned the margins in gold: "Abraham the Jew, Prince, Priest, Levite, Astrologer, Philosopher of the Jewish Nation, shall with the Eye of God disperse the Gauls. All Hail. DI." The document was signed by Nicolas Flamel and dated 1357. I crawled down another column and saw different crosses: Ankh, Greek, Latin, Patriarchal, Tao, Saint Andrew, Maltese, Potent . . .

I fell softly to the floor. The brotherhood took their domino-shaped togas from out of a chest, they had hooked crosses on their breasts. Caterpillars had no right to wear them.

Solange raised a steaming retort and recited:

Having existed for all eternity.
I was never born
of a father, or a mother,
but of an elemental
force of Nature:
of the branches of the trees,
the fruits of the forests,
the flowers of the mountain.

I have played in the night,
I have slept in the dawn.
I have been the viper in the swamp,
the eagle on the peaks,
the wolf in the forest.

I wandered at length over the earth
until I acquired Science,
and I have lived in a hundred worlds,
and moved in a hundred circles.

The chorus of moths replied:

We raised the dolmens and the menhirs
at the dawn of time; before Chartres

was, we raised the standard
of the Carnutes.

We shall exterminate the enemies of the pure race
with fire whose ashes will fall into the sea.

Before the Celtic invaders, before the Aryans,
in the golden Megalithic Age, we ruled.

We shall return . . . We shall return . . .
Any who oppose us
shall burn on the pyre, the mother of purity.

They lit black candles. Solange shoved her arm right up to the elbow into a wicker basket and removed a serpent, which gently and gracefully wrapped itself around her neck. I remembered the little snakes we used to play with on the estate and felt nostalgia for Eden. The initiated took turns drinking from a jar and after going into a trance fell to the floor in a flurry of seizing limbs. The crucial moment for Lazare had come, so the caterpillars were told to leave.

"They amuse me," Jules said.

"What will happen to Lazare?" I asked.

"If they kill him, he will come back to life."

Murky dawn light streamed in through the portholes.

"What did the Initiates drink?"

"Juice of Mandrácula."

They rejoined us an hour later.

Sabine and Jules

Jules invited me to his home. "Don't get excited, it's not a castle." He shared a large apartment with his sister and brother-in-law. I lived there for a while, it was close to the Institute of Psychology. Of course, I brought Bertha with me. Sabine told me that they actually did own a large castle, but they rented it out to the municipality, who paid well. Sabine de Saint-Germain was "different." Beautiful in her youth, a bone condition had given her a pronounced humpback. She now walked along looking at the ground as though she were searching for something impossible to find. But she was so intelligent and refined that it was a true relief to be with her. She made all the conversation and always kept up to date with the latest in art and literature.

She was more informative than a specialist magazine. Friendly, mischievous, ironic, Sabine was my friend.

Jules had turned thirty-two but looked eighteen. I can see him now: as refined as Sabine but somewhat melancholy, he adored wood and precious metals. For hours and hours, the two of us would glory in the dramatic enamels of churches, Italian stained glass, and Sevres-Limoges porcelain. A halo of wax and musk adorned Jules's head, I had never met anyone like him and never shall again. He was as smart as he was refined. Even though he was fond of silk shirts with lace cuffs and velvet suits, he never seemed anachronistic, and certainly not ridiculous.

"When I tire of myself, I shall commit suicide."

He would practice his "Argentine" with me, believing that it sounded better than Spanish, which he thought sounded "ordinary."

"Chela, I'd marry you. You're a great kid, you know?"

"I've never considered marrying," I lied.

August 1949. We'd go to Madrid: I had won a novel competition there. A few pesetas were involved, and that was always welcome. Jules, Bertha, and I made the trip. The sky of a Spanish summer. The bluest in Europe. The sky in Italy is radiant, but in Spain it's like a votive medallion. We went to Retiro to see the statues, we went up to the esplanade where, before the republic, only the king and his court were allowed to tread. Walking back down Avenida José Antonio, we browsed the picturesque stores and passed the Fountain of Cybele. The aromatic city reminded me of the linden blossom in La Plata. The Madrid version, however, was flavored with exotic spirits from the Levant.

And so we took our vacation from the attic, submitting to an enchanting tyrant: idleness. Sitting on the grass in the gardens around the Prado, we waited for it to open, bought tickets and went straight to the Goya gallery. *Chela, these are portraits of us, you at seventy and me at a hundred,* whispered Jules. Old people eating. Anointed in the water in the mirror of the rotunda in *Las Meninas,* we joined the family of Philip IV. The infanta Margarita reminded me of Lula, the only normal child, and the dwarves of Juan Sebastián. The characters in the royal painting seemed to step out of the frame so they could wander around the Hieronymites' original Prado.

When the city began to cool in October, we went to the publisher and I thought of Mr. Roux and my mother. In a horrible dive bar, we spoke to the editor.

"The first edition has sold out."

"People liked it?"

"Evidently."

"What did you do with the pesetas?"

"Do you know the author?"

Luis's elbow jabbed me in the ribs and I was filled with a compassionate light because, after all, this old man was a gentleman, like all Spaniards.

"We'll take some copies, if you have any left?"

"What will you tell her?"

"That the book disappeared up someone's ass."

Jules couldn't understand why the Spanish gentleman got angry, but then he wasn't very au fait with rude words in Spanish.

Jules suggested we make a film about the experience.

"We can set it in our castle."

"It's rented."

"We'll evict the tenants . . ."

To know that he was looking out for me almost brought me to tears. I said no.

We drank chamomile tea at the Manila de la Avenida bar and went to the Prado. Near a window overlooking the park sleeps a pink marble Ariadne. Nothing can upset her now, not fire or arrows, and her bronze bed is a long way from the Cretan Bull and the Minotaur. She no longer fears the monsters. I stroked her smooth feet, widowed now of feeling, with their slightly blue, bloodless veins.

"I wouldn't be unfaithful like Theseus," Jules exclaimed.

"We are the descendants of the Bull and the Minotaur, even

Scylla and Charybdis maybe. Our monstrous bloodline needs to be severed."

We could have been perfect, but humanity doesn't lend itself to perfection, and some misfortune was bound to crush us sooner or later.

We talked about the Louvre and the treasure resting in a stairwell, its torso trying to soar upward, the perfectly rendered belt and tunic damp with the waters of the Mediterranean. Such perfection in a fragile object drew the wrath of the gods. She was beheaded. Now she can't be sullied by moss or soot, but no one will know the beauty of her face and hair. When she was whole, she presided over the cosmic dance in honor of the Cabeiri on the island of Samothrace. Who gave the order to mutilate perfection?

If Mother Nature had obeyed the alchemists: "Mother Nature, don't sleep, do not produce simple creatures and base matter such as tin, gravel, and other vulgarities: embrace the great formulae that drive you to make gold, precious stones, and demigods." If Mother Nature hadn't looked the other way, today scholars would be asking for the following books and authors in stores and libraries: *Aurifontina Chymica*, *The Light Surging of Itself*, Basilius Valentinus, Roger Bacon, Ramon Llull, Nicolas Flamel, Arnaldus de Villa Nova, Morien, Lavimus, Trismosin, Philalethes, de Soucy.

My little tortoise slept in my pocket and poked out her head and feet when we spoke. I surmised that she was yearning for an idyllic time when she was gigantic and had a huge translucent shell, like charred honey. Bertha, my only tie to the Buenos Aires estate, poked my thigh and I stroked her back. We shared conferences, concerts, and museums, she kept me company on my most tragic days and it is only right for me to mention her now before moving on with my story.

It happened in the Louvre, on the blue and white rhombuses of the Caryatids courtyard. I put Bertha on the lovely floor and she started to crawl straight to a certain spot. She stopped in front of a statue of a Greek girl who was some way removed from her sisters in the Acropoli and lifted her rugged head as far as it would go. Her cheeks began to twinkle. Bertha was crying over impossible beauty. I said to her, "Don't cry, Bertha, neither you nor I will ever please the gods enough for them to grant us the grace of this girl in her long tunic."

Another Return

We went back to Paris the next day. I collected my mail and found a letter and a telegram. In the letter, Ariel informed me of an expropriation order; the Peronist people's government would pay me twice the value of the land, which he believed fair, because the lot had been allocated for a retirement home. The letter had been sent two months ago and the urgent telegram two days earlier. I decided not to start classes and to return immediately.

I arrived at the estate on September 5. Ariel tried to explain an endless of list of things that I couldn't understand. I was supposed to go to Governor Mercante's office.

"Is there no way to stop this?"

"No."

Peronism had taken away the last of my belongings. I gave Ariel power of attorney. In my anger I sought refuge in the attic. Sara came up just as before. But now she had opinions.

"What do you need so much land for when you live in France?"

The world had been turned on its head . . . Even Sara was thinking for herself. Not just thinking but indulging in discourse about politics, unions, the Basic Income, saying that no one should be too rich or too poor. I looked at the maid. Oh, no . . . this wasn't her. She'd ironed her hair and was wearing makeup.

"You're not losing anything, you get double the value. You people were never charitable, you never helped the poor," she murmured as she served the food.

She wanted to say something more, but didn't dare.

"Out with it, maid."

"The abuse has come to an end . . . Mr. Arnaldo is a representative, he's very busy organizing things."

I hated her just as much as the day she forgot my birthday. She started to make demands about back wages, and something involving the workers' union. She showed me some accounts. I was in debt to this piece of trash. I wrote a check for double what she was asking.

"If you trouble me again, I'll have you thrown out onto the street, you worthless scum."

She trembled at the reappearance of the little beast who had
so tormented her. I felt as though I were on the operating table,
having something removed. I went out to the fields to visit the
final frontier, the ruins of La Angelina. What did I care about
retirement homes? The Portuguese who bought their land from
Lula tried to talk to me, I didn't give them a chance. I wandered
around La Angelina for hours. I pulled up the horrible sign an-
nouncing the expropriation and scratched myself with the nails.
I kicked it and this time I hurt my foot. I'd go back to Europe.

Ariel was waiting for me in the grand hall with a package
and papers to sign:

"I was able to arrange everything. Look: they pay on time.
The law is severe but it's the law."

The soul of my people in paper money.

"When do they start?" I asked in anguish.

"Immediately," he said enthusiastically. "This government
thinks that actions speak louder than words, and they believe in
finishing the job."

"You don't know how painful this is for me."

"You need to get with the times, Chela."

"I'm not backward, you know that."

"You may live in Paris, but you're further behind than
Sara."

The Invasion

I went up to the attic and said to Bertha, "Things are craa-zee in the people house." Bertha ate Argentine lettuce with more relish than the French variety. I looked at the figurines we'd found. I heard an arpeggio ring out in the familial mist. A pavane for a sleeping child, for a dead child. The Manila shawl fell and the archangel shivering in the nude was a dead little boy.

From the historic chest I took a volume from the eighteenth century and read for hours. *Keys to Open Your Heart*. To make matters worse, I thought of Luis.

I spent a month in the attic, in the same place as before, with the same papers and objects. Just like before, Sara brought me a ham-and-cheese sandwich and a glass of juice that tasted of piss when it got warm.

One night, I was woken by clucking, as though there were a chicken coop downstairs. I spied the way I had on my mother and Mr. Roux. Six matrons, led by Sara, were drinking tea out of my porcelain, dipping their muzzles into century-old cups. I controlled myself. I'd explode later.

I confronted Ariel:

"You allow this atrocity?"

"It's of no great importance, Chela, they're flesh and blood . . ."

"How much severance do I have to pay Sara? I don't want her on the estate anymore."

Ariel was shocked and crossed himself. Arnaldo arrived, trying to calm things down. His lack of tact made me angrier still.

"Are you going to join the party, cousin?"

I dragged him to the door so determinedly that the bastard thought I had a gun. He fled our incomprehensible jungle. I made my arrangements at the agency where they knew me. I went for lunch at the old restaurant with Bertha in my pocket. I still have the napkin from that day. We were placed in a section where we could observe the restaurant without being seen ourselves. I sensed what was coming. Luis came in and stood in the middle of the dining hall. I spied in my habitual way. He didn't order anything, was he waiting for someone? A young woman came in, short and fat with acne all over her face. I saw her buttery hands cling to my beloved's blue pinstripe sleeves. She spoke in a shrill, childish voice, the kind you hear at the market, or at school.

She must be a teacher, I thought.

He dabbed at one of her oozing pimples with his handkerchief and the air filled with the scent of my despair. He stretched a protective arm around the back of her chair and rested his hand on her chubby neck. Oh, yes . . . they made a good couple.

"Let's go," I said to Bertha. I slipped her into my pocket and we scuttled out through a side door.

Out on the street, it burned like every desert in the world. My dead suddenly fell upon me like enormous icicles. My only hope had been thwarted by an idiot girl. "Too much theft, too much expropriation," I said to Bertha. I took a couple of pills from the blue bottle and soon I was smiling. We went into the usual café, I ordered a strawberry ice cream. I didn't ask them to play "La Violetera" because people didn't request songs there anymore. I stroked Bertha. "We're completely free, the two of us."

Back at the house, I called Sara.

"Tell me, how much severance do I owe you?"

She did sums in a little book. I wrote her a check for twice the amount.

"That's enough for a prefab. I'm leaving tomorrow."

"You'll leave right now."

She said her goodbyes from between a pair of suitcases, with a small, fragile parcel in her hands.

"What's in the parcel?"

"Miss Chela, please . . ."

I unwrapped it. Vomit rose up my throat. The boisterous slatterns had drunk their tea from this cup. When I was a child washing objects from the display case in my tub, I had made soapy waves and rubbed the cups from which their disgusting maws had supped, the handles their nasty trotters had grabbed hold of, I had waved these cups in the air.

The foam fell down upon me.

Paris Calling

Jules cabled; he'd heard about the political changes in the country and asked whether I was coming back or would be leaving my assistant's job at the Institute. He also said that Solange was gravely ill. I told him I'd be back in early December. I arrived in Paris on the third. I could now live off my savings without having to work. Bertha and I moved in to the attic in Saint-Germain and I felt like throwing away my flea-ridden rags the way Rimbaud had thrown out his from the garret given to him by Théodore de Banville.

Jules's butler brought drinks and food to me in my exile. Jules spent almost every afternoon and night with me. He brought a clavichord.

"String music, *mon ami*?"

"This clavichord belonged to my Saint-Germain ancestor, the Lord of Bell-Isle, bastard son of Frederick II Rackezi. He bought it in Germany during Louis XV's reign."

Jules warmed the cold evening with seventeenth-century strings lashed with metal tongues. He wore a tight-fitting Harlequin outfit made from Spanish corduroy, and lace cuffs. He decided that he would sleep in my attic. They brought up a bed that was just like mine, made from wood covered in gold leaf that was blood red where the gilt had flaked away. Bertha slept in an old Limoges soap dish, her legs and head dangling in the air.

We made a fire on top of a tripod, added incense and bay leaves, and the smoke clouded the glass opaline. Flowers of evil bloomed on the walls.

"My ancestor discovered the Fountain of Youth."

Symbols on the iron chests—of which there were two— indicated the existence of a continent that no longer appeared on any map. Perhaps it contained the Fountain of Youth?

"He was an extraordinary guy, he made the Philosopher's Stone as well," Jules continued.

Many marvels were contained in this attic. The entire Saint-Germain apartment was a museum. The motifs on the lampshades were Rosicrucian ovals, with preening pelicans and chicks that had been cheeping for three hundred years. The Cross of Saint Andrew, finished with roses, the Star of David spinning backwards, and on a shelf a little gold skeleton that fit in your hand. It had been made bone by bone, with Greek words visible in the joints.

"How wonderful."

"My ancestor made it by rubbing a small wooden skeleton with the philosopher's stone."

Sabine told me that Solange was refusing medical treatment. There were complications with her pregnancy and she had a miscarriage in her sixth month.

"What time did she die?"

"At six in the evening."

We took Sabine's car to the land of the Carnutes; it would be the last time we saw Solange.

Sabine, in dark glasses, looked like one of the dolls people "hang" from Christmas trees. Remus cried by her side. It was December 23. People disappeared after the gifts, the celebration, and the mistletoe. I imagined they'd hold the wake for Solange in the Caveau and we did indeed head to the dome above the pavilion.

When I entered, I read "Caveau." She looked like a dead princess. The mourning decorations decreed by the grandmother covered the engravings and symbols on the columns in crisp fabric and so Solange's universe disappeared into shadow. The voice of the priest, an uncle from the Taliesen Flamels, intoned the slow requiem and from the grand hall on the ground floor rose music from the seventeenth century.

When the priest left, the grandmother placed a fetus wrapped in red silk printed with the three profiles of the family crest in the arms of the young mother. The last of the Taliesin Flamels had escaped the horror of growing up an inbred ogre with a grotesque head.

No one could save the dolphin from the river now.

I felt a tremendous yearning for the warmth of home, for someone of my blood somewhere in Italy, to uncover the roots of my anguish. I would expose myself to the ancestral beast even if she ripped out my belly. Perhaps I was leaving Solange's wake only to head for my own?

I left without saying goodbye to anyone. They'd think it was "just another of Chela's crazy whims," and would bury me along with Solange and her incestuous little child.

Rome

My absolute autonomy was the kind bought by money and exile. At six in the morning, I took a train to Rome. On the journey I felt that the universe revolved around me, I was ready to take the family bull by the horns.

Successful or not, whatever happened, I was living in a state of constant awareness. I spent my days in inquiry, analysis, and interpretation and when I grew tired I went for long walks.

Rimbaud once wrote: *Perhaps you're right about reading and walking a lot. It is in any case a reason not to lock yourself up in offices and the family home. The brutalization should occur far from those places.* I was fleeing from the home of the Saint-Germains on my way to who knows what manner of brutality.

I lodged at the Minerva Hotel in Rome. I lay down

wondering how my life would be if I weren't quite so fanci-
ful, what might have become of me if I had been so crammed
with objectivity that there was no room left for the imagination.
And especially, what this familial reject might have been if she
hadn't been gifted with extreme intelligence.

Now I needed the embrace of family. Yes, Luis had softened
me. I would walk, dig, stride, hop, and sit on a bench along the
way to remove my thorns, like Fedele, the Boy with Thorn.
What was all this truly about? Searching for something of Luis
in every man who crossed my path: a gesture, a scent, the smell
of his cigarettes. I was behaving like a seventeenth-century
dandy. And such harm it did me searching for these subtle ab-
surdities, trying to put together a crazy puzzle whose pieces
never fit: his brand of tobacco, the soft feel of his handkerchiefs,
the golden brooch he gave me one November afternoon, a silly
trinket that I even took to bed with me but lost when the clasp
broke from wear.

One night, in Rome, I committed my greatest gaffe. I ran to
hug an elegantly dressed gentleman smoking in a distinctively
apathetic way. "I'm sorry not to be him," he said to me. Was it
my only wish to marry Luis? My absolute freedom allowed me
to sleep with whomever I wanted, but Luis had castrated me. A
sexual act with someone else would be a betrayal, something
dirty. I tried to conjure the image of September in my homeland
by the Rio de la Plata, with some kids playing football by the

shore in spring, near the outcrop. Lying awake all night was a torment, so I resorted to sleeping pills.

I transferred my money to an Italian bank. I spent little. I became the dirty country girl once more, wandering around in crumpled pants, shirts in carelessly chosen colors, sneakers, and my hair tied up in a pair of braids. I was thirty, but I looked twenty-two. I was just another bum, or one of the many unfortunate children of the postwar period. I spent a year living in Rome without making friends or going to any kind of event or conference, because the cultural life in Paris had worn me out. To eat, I'd get a drink and a sandwich, lettuce for Bertha, and thus passed my days in Rome.

I went down into the catacombs, which are like inverted attics, the opposite of what you find in houses, and in their sinister, intimate atmosphere the ingenuous paintings showed me the infancy of my religion. I saw Laocoön in the Vatican Museum and would have liked to take Aesthetics again, at the Faculty of Humanities, with Guerrero.

I found so much greatness suffocating, the greatness of the city of the Caesars, which slips into every orifice, every pore of one's body, or soul, through the windows of a bus, the eye of a lock, every shop window.

It happened in front of Michelangelo's *Pietá*. I thought I was going to die. What would happen to Bertha if I died suddenly?

No one knew where the human debris I had become was. I woke up in a hospital on the Via Veneto.

Yes, Bertha was in the soap dish on the nightstand.

I had contracted malaria and was given quinine and antibiotics. The Argentine Consulate was informed. They asked if I had family in Rome. As though speaking from underwater, I gasped, "In Sicily."

I recovered, but ever since I have suffered sporadically from extremely annoying fevers.

After a month in hospital, I was thrilled to be discharged. A nurse walked me to the station to buy a ticket for Sicily.

Caserta

January 1953. I sent a telegram to Borgo Stradolini de Caserta: Messina. "For my great-aunt Angelina." It was like throwing a message in a bottle into the sea.

At the station in Rome, I asked whether they offered discounts and for two hundred lira I was able to travel first class. We left at six that freezing morning. Having slept for a couple of hours, I woke up in Naples. Waiting for my next transfer, I ate macaroons and cheese, and drank a little Chianti. Bertha ate her usual meal and was happy. I fell asleep on the next train and woke again in Calabria to the sound of the Sicilian packet boat's horn.

I was soon surrounded by locals from the island. They were mostly gaunt with curly hair. My father's eyes stared out from

every face. They were generous and shared a delicate but fla-
vorful piece of goat's cheese and a little Messina wine in a tin
cup; they knew I was a foreigner and were curious.

I told them I was going to Borgo and they asked whether it
was for work. They assumed that I must be a servant. My pants,
the second pair I'd bought, had got sullied during the long journey, and combined with the sneakers and a ponytail made me
look quite wretched. I was a tramp. I remembered the advice I
got from a nurse at the hospital: "Acqua e sapone."

They continued to ask questions, wondering whether I was
French. I think I have that look. We trooped down the gang-
plank. Messina. I looked for a hotel. I would delay my arrival
in Borgo for as long as possible. I was struck by the sweltering
atmosphere, thick with olive oil. Thick dust stuck to my skin,
redolent with citrus and spice aromas. There was a small hotel
on the road to Borgo run by three women: Cloto, Laquesis, and
Atropos. Somewhere farther away, another woman sang what
sounded like a Cretan air.

Exhaustion sent me tumbling onto a red divan in a pink
lobby. A print of a saint with her breasts cut off bled down onto
my head from the wall.

"Would you like one of Saint Agatha's breasts?" asked one
of the women.

Candy in the shape of severed breasts, dripping with crim-
son sugar. On this island, even the sweets were tragic.

"Thank you, I'm not sure I want a breast."

"Are you on your own? Are you staying for long?"

I understood the dialect and knew that they were wary of me; because the wars hadn't awoken the folk of Messina, they couldn't conceive of a woman traveling alone.

"Do you have a room with a bathroom?"

"Come, you can wash here."

I washed in stages in an outdoor basin, and dried myself. It was freezing.

"Where's the toilet?"

They brought an enormous bucket.

"Come, do it here, here, don't worry."

But they stood there like scarecrows, watching.

"Are you going to Borgo for work?"

"No, to live."

"You're going to live there, inside?"

"Yes."

Their attitude changed.

"Come inside, miss. We'll bring wine and sardines."

I drank plenty of wine because the sardines made me thirsty. In the bedroom was a bed with a very white blanket, a table with a glass, and an image of Saint Agatha inside a little glass dome. The sight made me think of Lula. What had become of her?

Bertha slept on a pillow, she had eaten and was happy to be

on an adventure. She loved change. Tomorrow, I would ask the youngest woman to go to Borgo to have them come pick me up. I was tired.

The message in the bottle had reached its destination. A car was sent from Borgo, as old as the one back at the estate in Argentina. It was driven by Vittorio, my great-aunt's chauffeur and gardener.

I'd learned some things about life "inside" from the gossip of Cloto, Laquesis, and Atropos. For example, that my great-aunt owned the sulfur mines that dyed the air yellow and the olive groves that made it sticky, a chain of stores specializing in silk made by Angelina's worms, which she also exported to the continent, a cinema, and several Californian-style apartment complexes. I shivered and Vittorio noticed.

"*Freddo*, eh?"

I looked out at the sparsely vegetated landscape. Sculptures appeared here and there in the grass. The stonemasons took off their caps and hailed us.

"Your father was Madam Angelina's nephew?"

"Yes."

"Then Miss is her great niece, the only one?"

"I have a sister who's a nun."

"*Morta* . . ."

"Why do you say that?"

"The world is hidden from her, she's *morta*."

"She's very pretty, Vittorio."

"As I said, *morta*."

Sicilian conversation: wry and to the point.

Vittorio continued his blunt summation.

"You were Spanish before."

"What's my great-aunt like?" I asked, breaking the subsequent silence.

"She doesn't go out much."

I could now see that the sculptures had large heads.

"What are the statues of?"

"They're stone."

"Is my aunt married?"

"She's a *signora*."

We walked into a patio with red tiles. Inside the stables, the flagstones had been broken long ago by knights mounting their steeds. Vittorio parked the car where a sawhorse nibbled at the end of a stake. The tiles were loose in places, just like at the old Angelina, where I'd made my find. In the front courtyard were reliefs of our ancestors with the names underneath each portrait. Our surname hadn't changed since 1200. Underneath a Spanish balcony I read the epic inscription:

"The Stradolini lived in Messana, previously known as Zancle, before the Carthaginian invasion and fought the Mamertines to the death in Rome. The bloodline joined the cream of Spanish nobility in the early eighth century: they fought with Spain against the Arabs of Mauritania. Constables of Caserta have founded academies and villas."

Fernando Stradolini e Ucelli de Caserta and María Gertrudis della Rovere e Ucelli de Caserta were beautiful, but they did not reproduce well. They were surrounded by big-headed offspring.

I could have spent the whole day exploring the exteriors and the walls. In a niche was the family coat of arms: the portrait of Fernando was framed by a kind of dragon. On the tressure was a blue lis against a white background along with the standard of Saint Dionysius. All the fountains and troughs were garlanded with the dragon's flames.

I found a spiral staircase that rose up to a terrace. I climbed up and saw forests, the *cortili* passages cut into the stone, rising clouds of sulfur, and smokestacks from kitchens brightening the afternoon with trays of fried food.

"Miss, in Rendazzo there are *castellos* as big as the house of God, in Taormina there's one with a golden staircase."

"Who are you?"

"No one, miss. My name is Truppi Cagliero, from the Pagliari del Borgo."

"Why do you say you are no one? You're Truppi Cagliero."

"Miss sounds like a Communist."

I explained to him that I was no Communist, but then remembered the business with Sara. I shouldn't have been surprised.

"What's Lady Angelina like?"

"She's a lady."

A hundred wars wouldn't change the Sicilians.

Oh yes, something stank. Perhaps it was we, the reaction-aries, who were crumbling away? Leaning on the small tower rising from the terrace, I fingered the musical skin of a shepherd's pipes, the hide of a bleating flock, the resonant epidermis of a mandolin, all dyed a sulfurous yellow.

The Ancestors

As I watched, the mist swept over and hid Cape Faro from sight, embroidering Aspromonte in lace strewn here and there with sparkling bursts of light.

Peach buds began to surge forth in the orchard and when summer arrived the sap would heat up the trunk and the river would begin to flow. On my Buenos Aires plains, the winter did not silence nature. Here, life went quiet, the only creatures that stirred were the shepherd waking his sheep and goats and their few offspring. Then the animals would trot around nibbling at plants, releasing the lonely fragrance of thyme, whose spines cleave the air, arousing a kind of pity.

"Miss, would you like to clean up a little before you see

Lady Angelina? I am Truppi Carmela, the housemaid," she said, introducing herself because she was someone.

She was the daughter of old Pagliari del Borgo.

"What do the statues in the low fields mean, what do they represent?"

"Yes . . . they're funny."

"Is my great-aunt asleep?"

"I don't know, miss."

"But you're the housemaid."

"The one who knows is Imperatore Ágata, the maid of the bedchamber."

The shower, which was freezing at times, perked me up. Washed and dressed, I went down to the grand hall.

The walls were clad in wood paneling that at intervals opened into ovals to frame ninety-seven portraits of ancestors. Behind an enormous pair of breasts appeared Imperatore Ágata.

"My dear mistress, how are you? Lady Angelina is on her way."

We sat around a table whose legs were carved into lions clasping globes. There's a similar one in a portrait at the Prado. Charles II resting his feathered hat on a table. There was a portrait of Philip IV and Lady Marianne of Austria. The boy looked scrawny, sickly, and not very bright. There was a genuine Antonello: the painter's signature, from 1400, was very clear. I learned that my aunt had saved the painting for Borgo, winning out over vultures and museums. There was a portrait of Duke Uccelli of Caserta.

As regards the portrait by Antonello of Messina, later my great-aunt would tell me about how she fought to obtain it due to the fact that a Della Rovere (from the Urbino branch of the family) visited the painter's father and later took charge of the studies of the son, who went on to be a disciple of Colantonio.

A determined scholar of everything family-related, Angelina found out that as a teenager Antonello rode with Rovere Uccelli in Flanders, Rome, and Reggio Calabria.

She believed that we were related to Antonello of Messina. There's another self-portrait of Antonello in a museum in London.

I have exchanged one memory for another, the canvas with the face of the Sicilian artist for the one I saw freed from the tomb on the shoulders of his savior.

I have exchanged one time for another, the ugly creature I have become is cold and stirs the logs in the iron stove while also stirring up the fire in the stove in Borgo.

Red flames warmed the room, giving the darkness a warm hue. The hall was similar to the one painted behind the feathered silhouette of Charles II; in other words, it had the deathly magic of the Hall of Mirrors in the Palace of Buen Retiro. There was a fragment of a mural of musical angels. The other half is in the Bellomo Palace in Syracuse.

On the main wall, the Constable of Caserta sat astride a horse, without his family, wearing armor and a sash and holding the standard of his rank. On another wall, a knight in full armor was brandishing a sword during a battle in a ravaged wooded landscape, with gusts of leaves forcing birds to flee south. In the distance, one could see a *castello* with crenellated towers and a squire with a lance. An ermine sniffed the leg of the knight, Duke Francisco María della Rovere.

On a gold table was a stucco medallion with a portrait of María Antonia of the Two Sicilies, daughter of Frances I and relative of Charles IV of Spain.

There were two display cases of clocks and bells, lovers climbing up a Neapolitan vase, a pear-shaped lute, under a Manila shawl was a harp just like the one in my attic.

On the table, the breasts of Imperatore Ágata rested comfortably, protected by a lace covering. Half-asleep, she occasionally started awake and looked toward the door.

In my large pocket, Bertha ate lettuce next to the figurine we'd found. I would ask Angelina about the large-headed figures in the field. I didn't mind having to wait.

I inspected a stylized case containing crowns and swords from the eighteenth century, precious stones, and an ivory Last

Supper. Behind me, something was happening. Ágata had stood up. I turned around but didn't see anyone.

And yet she was there.

When I saw her, I said to myself, *I've seen this before.*

It was during an excursion to Mantua, in the Duke's Palace, on the canvas in the Overtari Chapel portraying a gathering of the court of Juan Francisco Gonzaga, the protector of Andrés Mantegna, who was entrusted with decorating the couple's bedchamber.

I greeted my great-aunt but my mind continued to think back . . . a man dressed in scarlet was delivering a letter to Francisco. Under the sofa of the future cardinal was a lovely dog, the interlocutors were surrounded by ladies and gentlemen. Near Isabel . . . were the little people. I saw one protected by the mantle of Isabella d'Este.

The little woman declared how happy she was that I had come, offering many words of welcome while Ágata laid the table for a meal. There was a pleasant smell of yawning coffers full of apples and lavender. Ágata brought an album and Angelina handed me a photograph of a little girl dressed in organdy. That horrible day, the day on which my mother died in my soul, fell upon me.

"This little girl is the daughter of my nephew Stradolini in Argentina."

"*Per Dio . . .*" Ágata exclaimed, as though it were some extraordinary fact.

The only extraordinary one was Angelina, who to reach an ordinary dining table had to climb up seven steps and sit in a high chair.

She had good teeth and her strong Sicilian jaw chewed relentlessly. Her voice was hoarse with ancient chastity. She laughed happily, raising thick eyebrows over bulging eye sockets.

"*Poverella . . .*"

She stroked my cheek, out of pity or a protective impulse, I don't know. Now she was apologizing. "Forgive me, Chela," she said, pushing aside her cutlery and grabbing the fowl with her hand, rubbing bread in the sauce on her plate, quaffing wine like a gambler, eating two portions of dessert, and scraping the bottom of the pot of jam like a spoiled child.

Yes, we ate turkey, just like that time back at the house.

Finally, she puffed on a meerschaum pipe, its glowing red eye sparking intermittently to life. Empty, the plates revealed the family's dragon motif, our dessert wine sat sulfur yellow in our glasses.

Full, Angelina smoked, asking questions.

"Has your sister confined herself definitively?"

"Yes, with the Carmelites."

"Is she pretty?"

"Very pretty and very blond."

"She's one of ours . . ."

"My little brother died."

"I know. We're the only Stradolinis left in the world."

In the Family

"Chela has some Stradolini features, but she must look more like her mother," she said to Ágata.

She was right, I did look like my mother, but I didn't say so. Angelina slept like an ogress. I loved her.

I moved into the Borgo tower and Angelina climbed up the spiral staircase. We were the last remnants of a dying elite. We got to know each other. We liked each other.

Angelina was very intelligent. She had studied at a school for the children of nobility, and must have had to defend herself from her fellow pupils, who would have called her *testone ostinate* and similar. She excelled. Her aggression got her expelled and she was sent back to the people house. Her parents and four brothers couldn't bear to see her, her small size undermined the dignity of the group.

The wars laid waste to her family, and she went up to the attic.

"I am both a virgin and a widow."

She insisted on telling me about her private life. Thus I learned about how her father arranged a marriage with a cousin, Francisco Salina de Caserta, who, when he met her, stayed true to his commitment to marry but immediately fled off to war and died. Angelina fell in love.

She still kissed a portrait she treasured in an oval reliquary. Inspecting the image closely, I thought he looked like Marcelo Mastroianni.

She talked about the Fascists and the war: "I was more afraid of the Fascists than the bombing. I think the tragedy began with Garibaldi and continued with Mussolini. I mean the tragedy that beset the great families, which I think must have been planned by some of ours because the common swine would never have started anything on their own. They have a base, listless nature. And also because, deep down, they admire us and dream of sharing our towers. I blame the upper classes and the ideologues they create because the commoners are social climbers; they want to be aristocrats when they get to power but aristocrats are born with fine wrists and ankles that haven't done manual labor or raised livestock for centuries. It's in our blood."

She sounded like she was running for election. She would subject Bertha and me to long rants and speeches: "The commoners will fall back into the mud from which they came because everything always reverts to the natural plan and finds its ancestral level."

The house had been the target of attacks by Communists and socialists since 1860. Angelina wrote a lot about that and under fascism published articles under the pseudonym Diana Luppi. She told Bertha and me, "If my legs had been long enough, I'd have kicked the Duce in the head in Dongo."

I shall never forget the hours spent touring the castle interiors, the cold halls whose only warmth came from the tapestries and wood. It was a dark, fortified citadel and I followed old trails down passages and into bedrooms with empty four-poster beds adorned with the coat of arms on their canopies. I especially won't forget the smell of the island, like incense but not, like musk but not, neither animal nor vegetable. It got everywhere like a rancid gremlin.

I began to fall in love with the lady of the castle. My great-aunt had one foot on the ground and one foot in the family tree. Although she never left Borgo, she kept an eye on business via well-trained lackeys. One of them was Vittorio, who was charged with oversight of the sulfur mines and olive groves.

In addition to being the maid, Ágata oversaw the stores, the cinema, and one or two other concerns.

Vittorio affiliated himself with the Fascists to protect Borgo from expropriation and became one of the leaders of the movement. He, Asunta, and Ágata hid my aunt for quite a long time. I was quite surprised when I learned where . . .

My stay at Borgo gave me time to think and write. Angelina and I wrote for a newspaper in Naples, and Vittorio went to collect our payment at the end of every month. She moved into my attic permanently and we forgot about the world, ignoring both the day and the night, lit by wax candles and our love for each other. She dubbed me Francesco and I called her Luis. And so we experienced surprising, indescribable pleasures that today brand and scorch me like a red-hot iron.

These blasphemous deeds occurred in an atmosphere of childish bliss; the diminutive she-dragon gave me all the love denied to me by everyone else. Focusing on her, I could have everything I had wanted but was never given, and so we helped each other to love and be loved, enamored with our dreams, worries, failures, and solitude, engaged like accursed spirits in the sovereign enterprise of giving and receiving, a hopeless endeavor.

The act of love was all that interested us.

If we had been back at home, Sara would have shouted, "Dirty girls, why don't you wash?"

Ágata, in contrast, whispered, "It's such a warm morning, why not go for a swim in the bay?"

We went down and I swam like a fish. She blinked uncomfortably under an umbrella.

I was thirty, but looked twenty-two standing naked on the shingle. She stroked skin that clung tight to my frame like a swimming costume and we were coated in the ambiguous flavor of love.

"Dark . . . why? The Stradolinis have always been fair."

María Salomé, Lula, was blond, but I had inherited my mother's coloring, a smoky ivory, toasted opal.

"Would you have loved Lula more?"

"I've never loved anyone the way I love you."

We came together in forbidden love like two branches of a rotten tree. Orphans, lost and fallen into soft, tender mud that spread, swallowing us further, like a viscous, adorable sex. A murky pit of perspicacious eels learned in the art of satisfying our terrible, repressed appetites.

"You look like Goya's *Maja*," she said to me.

Ágata served us refreshments on the narrow beach bordered by outcrops that towered dark and imposing over the sand. Out of the caves, the lairs of monsters, ran lilac-blue water. The portholes of Borgo stared out from the hill, keeping an eye on the sculptures scattered like creatures in an unpleasant dream.

Ágata brought a silver tray on which wobbled a gelatine tower, red from the strawberry with an aroma of fragrant cinnamon, and a little marsala as is the wont of the islanders, but when she saw I was naked she withdrew. Her peasant soul would never understand.

Back in the attic I saw that Angelina's eyes were irritated and she had a livid scarlet bruise on her neck. I had my own battle wounds.

Angel, Angelina

She read all the newspapers. She had them sent from the continent.

"Perón's government is on its last legs," she told me.

I was happy to hear I might get back my land.

"The scum will have to tighten their belts, the way the commoners did after Mussolini," she went on.

Angelina taught me to bind books. She conserved her collections, treating them for moths and weevils, and kept her incunabula safe in chests. Her little hands folded, cut, twisted, and pasted with an arsenal of paper, glue, and other materials she imported from Barcelona, producing treasured texts that she placed on gleaming shelves of acacia and oak. She bound contemporary texts in leather, French texts in buckskin, Italians

in suede, and for Kafka and Joyce she made metallic zinc covers, as though she wanted to protect them from a fusillade of
bullets. I was surprised that she had included them, but later I
learned why.

She was extremely skilled at handling material that embel-
lished dreams and would often get impatient with me and snatch
away a piece I was messing up with my naturally clumsy hands.
With art and elegance, Angelina integrated the kingdom of fine
literature with the vegetable one of textiles, the animal realm
of skins, and the mineral domain of stone. In a small imperial
cabinet were incunabula protected with chenille and some very
small books containing ancient aphorisms whose covers spar-
kled with encrusted agates, her favorite stone. Their coloring
ranged from red to chocolate. She bound texts analyzing religion, revealing the truth about human nature, and one whose
cover was a garnet rose, a nineteenth-century French transla-
tion in which the chapters followed the cycles of the sexes to
their logical culmination. I copied out the following paragraph:
"WE were ALL once ONE, but because of our sins we were
separated into man and woman, dismantling the supreme har-
mony of androgyny."

In this book, I read that Homeric monsters really existed.
The author was a Greek who lived in Babylonia and he claimed
that these monsters live dormant inside of all of us, we are their
carriers as they await the right moment to reemerge. Then

humanity will show its true colors. Thus saints are doves and murderers Minotaurs, deformed hybrid creatures.

I'd like to write more about the contents of the imperial cabinet: lined up on two of the inner shelves were an abraxas with the head of a serpent; the Seven Apocalyptic Seals of Saint John; little crystal spheres for crystalmancy, a magic wand and a tripod for predicting the future; a large chalice-shaped glass for lecanomancy; and a pile of three bricks next to a volume by Diodorus Siculus, with Sargonic symbols.

We talked in the tower, sitting in the heart of the lilac-blue shade.

"You asked me why I kept Kafka and Joyce in the library? I didn't want to get rid of metamorphosis or weirdness because under fascism I was a hidden bug myself. Vittorio joined the party and swore on his honor that I had fled to London. But I was in there."

"There" resembled a huge cuckoo clock. I went closer to where she was pointing and saw that it was decorated with an engraving of a painting by Antonello, *Saint Jerome in His Cell*.

"It was my cell during that time, and from this lintel or that frieze I'd hear them singing and playing cards. I spied on them for years through a crack in the door."

Vittorio had put her away like a doll and she crept through a passage in the saint's study, closing the little red door behind her. She ran barefoot over the small leaf-green

rhombus-and-quadrilateral floor and leaned over the little balcony formed by the arch. She drew on her inner Jerome, sitting on the apologist's chair, staring at the moment at which he
signed the Vulgate. She could no longer hear the shouting and
laughter of the thugs, just the sound of the erudite pen of the
translator and the folios on the lectern.

. "Didn't you go crazy in there?"

"No. I entertained myself feeling the rough crystals. You
can't see them because they're inside. And I inspected the contents of retorts and bottles in which they age a liqueur drunk
by the children of the constables, seven dwarves, that makes
you forget everything except what you want to remember or
find out."

I showed her the sculpture I'd found in the stable yard,
which dated back to 1848; the big-headed sculptures on the island were derived from the mother sculpture. She asked me to
put her in the altarpiece the way Vittorio had. A little while
later, she asked me to take her out again.

She brought a couple of thimbles of liqueur, plenty for her,
not much for me. I drank the aged relic, it was cinnamon but
not vegetable, musk but not animal, topaz yellow but not mineral, and we both headed into the palace that has no doors or
windows.

A palace of ecstasy in which the Casertas appeared in all
their splendor and horror: princes mated with little women,

princesses with big-headed little men, and so we knew that our bloodline could never have thrived.

While we were there, Jerome himself came down and gave us the formula of the elixir a wizard had given to him which he passed on to the monks so they could take charge of and wield white magic, become familiar with red magic, identify green magic, and exorcise black magic. He told us that Silvester II had drunk too much of the elixir and learned too much, that alchemical formulae and spells are dangerous for those who aren't damaged in some way.

Ulysses

I don't know how long the journey lasted. When I got back, I had new wrinkles on my face and the hands of an eighty-year-old. My soul and body were terribly ravaged by age and since then I have moved like a worm. I had burned up my life. After that day, I have always felt as though someone or something were grabbing me by the hair.

"You know everything and more," said Angelina.

I needed to rest. Angelina gave me a boat beached on the shingle. She'd stay in Borgo and I would sail the seas like Ulysses.

In August 1955, I commenced my maritime adventure. At first, I kept close to the island but I didn't dare explore the caves of the glowworms. Tourist yachts were making the same voyage: I sailed down the Strait of Messina and headed toward the Tyrrhenian Sea, passing Palermo and Trapani, or out into the Mediterranean past Syracuse and Catania.

Message in a Bottle

I became friendly with a family of sailors by the name of Campobaso who had made their fortune selling wire on the continent. I'd never tell Angelina about my involvement with such commoners. My boat, the *Barracuda*, needed someone to clean it and I needed someone to cook, so I invited the Campobasos to sail with me. They would perform these tasks.

Carmelo, the father, was an expert diver. The Sicilian coast was visible from the *Barracuda*. When we decided to go so far it was lost from sight, we hired a pilot from Syracuse. One morning, Carmelo cried out on his return from the seabed, "A ship, a sunken ship."

We went to the prefecture of Palermo to report the find and they promised to go without fail that afternoon. So we had to wait a week. Finally, they appeared with specialized staff, nets, cranes, and a lot of diving equipment.

Objects came up in baskets: a figurine in black and red ceramic, a winged gorgon with snakes sprouting from her forehead, legs bent in readiness to leap into flight, arms like oars, and the ugly face of an Assyrian god; a collection of metallic objects including two gold hoop earrings in the shape of a sun whose rays were finished in pearls with excellent nacre; a necklace in the shape of an olive branch up which a cherub climbed; several bronze bowls and silver mirrors; a silver lamp with Etruscan motifs; and the ship's bell with the name of the vessel etched into it: *Lucania*.

To refloat it, American experts were called in. And so we saw the trireme whose log, kept safe from the water in a coffer, told us that the *Lucania* had sailed the seas from Gaul to Greater Greece.

We wondered what they had been doing, whether their mission was trade, or whether they were lucomos with purple robes and ivory chairs. Evidently an Attic slave had copied etchings of untranslatable Etruscan symbols and combined them with those from his homeland, unaware that in doing so he was prefiguring the Florentine renaissance at a time that predated the Parthenon. The same artisan had seemingly also forged cups from Corinth, because within classical Greek meanders there suddenly stirred restless etchings of tails that undermined Aegean serenity: a fiery Italian temperament burned within this Athenian fret.

The ship's log indicated a course. "Sybaris, stopping at the port, return to the Peloponnese, follow the path of the water, stop at Carthage" was written in Greek. A page in the same language told of a sailor's homesickness: the lovely architecture, the atrium, tiles decorated with birds and fish, the family tombs and the children he might never see again. The *Lucania* was scuttled on the orders of the captain so as not to reveal the route to pirates.

We found an iron gate that led into the belly of the trireme; the Americans pulled on the ring and it opened with a sigh of putrid air. Even the Americans were startled. A woman slept, frozen in a cry of terror that only now was finally released, letting out centuries of horror.

She wasn't mentioned in the log so we consulted the ship's manifest: "A captain, a boatswain, second boatswain, eight marines, a scribe, eight seamen, thirty crossbowmen, and one hundred and fifty-six oarsmen." There was nothing about a woman who was now a skeleton sitting dark and untouched, fragile as a piece of black coral.

She had spent centuries in her curule seat, which had been decomposing for years. I thought that if Aphrodite had a skeleton, this is what it would look like. The experts took measurements: "Small calvaria, smooth jawbones, Olympian forehead," and decided that she couldn't be Etruscan given the long bones and height of five foot six. On the ring finger of the left hand, she had a ring that one of the Americans slipped off and gave to me as a present. It fit perfectly and I felt a caress from across the ages. I inspected the jewel and made out a gold base and a blurry crest under the enamel.

She couldn't have been Etruscan, the objects in her bedroom indicated a different background: glass and powdered marble cups and chalices, not *bucchero nero* ceramics. Boxes with gold inlay, silver crowns, and cameos of Minerva Partenos suggested that the lady had been Greek. In contrast, the captain's jewel box contained soothsayers' symbols from Etruria in the shapes of crows, goshawks, cranes, owls, parrots, weasels, and grasshoppers. While the captain may have been guided by magical symbols, the lady followed the Rhombus. It slipped down from the chair; in life it would have hung from her neck.

"Bullroarer," said an American. He spun the Rhombus and we heard the Bullroarer-Bullroarer, the ritual music of the Mysteries of Dionysius. I played with it for a few minutes and heard Juan Sebastián's two words.

Soon afterward, I was struck down with malaria, treated with quinine, and recovered. The Americans gave me a few objects and kept many more. The *Lucania* would be brought to the Palermo ship museum and the lovely skeleton put on display in a museum of oddities.

Scorpion

When I got back to Borgo, I found that Angelina had damaged her health waiting for me on the beach for weeks on end, her face turned to the sun. In bed, her large head sank into the feather pillow and she looked up at me with the tragic expression of an Etruscan mask. Bertha was on her nightstand.

Guilt struck me like a scorpion's sting. I'd forgotten about them both while I was off on my buccaneering treasure hunt.

"The sun hurt her, just the same as when she was waiting for her husband," said Ágata.

"Here are the newspapers from your country, Perón is on the way out," said Angelina, rousing herself.

A photograph in *La Nación* showed the fires: the Santo Domingo and San Nicolás churches were burning. Others were now nothing more than ash and rubble. I swore I would make my own bonfire as soon as I returned.

Angelina recovered quickly, revived by her fascination with the discovery of the trireme. We went back up to the attic.

She asked to see the ring, she wanted to examine it for names and dates. She dipped it in a liquid that gave off red smoke. At the bottom of the chalice, the ring gave up dates, symbols, and letters. She picked up a magnifying glass to conclude her examination.

"It's not a date, it's a symbol."

Under a greenish patina, we read: "IL VIRI S.F." My great-aunt told me that this was an abbreviation for the names of the two High Initiates entrusted with guarding the Sybilline Books.

We read more: "DUUMVIRI FACIUNDIS." The little mouse shoved half her body into the imperial cabinet and removed a hermetic tome. She opened the lock with a little key, turned to a chapter, and began to explain.

"This woman, the lady from the ship, was a Cretan Sybil. Crete is in the middle of the Mediterranean and its central position made it an aquatic capital: the island's ships sailed the Mediterranean basin, reaching the Ionian Sea and the Aegean, getting as far as the Tyrrhenian and the Adriatic."

"Perhaps she was hired by the *Italiotas* to use her powers?" I asked.

"She was expelled from Crete when it fell under Roman regency, in which the Etruscans played a significant role. The material in the coffer is from the final years of the Roman monarchy, the period of Tarquin the Proud."

We worked seven days and seven nights in the attic and the ring continued to shed layers of grime. Angelina stirred the contents of the chalice with a wand that had a little star on the end, the kind you see in fairy tales. It looked innocent but it was based on a science the ignorant call superstition: the occult.

To perform the exercise, my great-aunt wore an ankle-length tunic, bonnet, and gloves, murmuring unintelligible spells while periodically pouring ancient-looking balsams that boiled without the need for heat. She studied the materials the Americans had given me and some of the grime-covered stones revealed reliefs, lovely profiles like the Parisienne fresco in Knossos.

The vessels of oil and perfume gave off essences used by the women of a defunct thalassocracy, when the tree of the West was little more than an acorn.

A stamp the lady used to sign documents and as a personal seal gave us her name: "Elida de Zancle de Caserta." Yes, I had felt our ancient ancestor calling to me from the belly of the trireme, and suddenly we were beset by concern about her final resting place.

"I shall see her buried in the Stradolini–Ucelli de Caserta necropolis," declared Angelina.

Angelina's influence was enough to overcome whatever protests were raised, and seven days layer Vittorio was carrying Elida de Zancle in a long box of the kind usually used to transport rolls of silk to and from the stores of Borgo. Vittorio was stony-faced and grouchy, he didn't like dealing with the dead. We started to work on the beautiful bones. We joined the smaller ones together with copper wire and the larger ones with a thicker kind we had to bend with pliers.

Seven days after that, *numero Deus*, she was sitting, smiling in her curule chair as though she were posing in a photography studio. Such a lovely skeleton would grace any tastefully decorated space. It was a shame to bury it. I hung the rhombus from her neck bones and it spun and spun like a dervish.

"We shall dress her in a Spanish cloak and tassels, hood, and buttoned tunic because she was born in Zancle, was educated in Crete, and married an Italian constable."

Although Elida was thoroughly pagan, she would have a Christian resting place. The chapel had been built before the Borgo castle and its simple design made it look like a Roman fort, with a square wooden tower rising from the rocks, a tree-trunk stockade, and parapeted entrance. Other bones rested in the chapel in the traditional manner of the time, on eternal flagstones. The remains blanched among beads, helmets, and armor. In some of them, I noticed the signs of our family affliction.

To find the right place for Elida de Zancle de Caserta, we climbed a spiral staircase up to the tower from whose round window one could see the imposing surroundings of the castle, the V-shaped open ditch, and a patio of red tiles like the one on our estate.

A chaplain from Messina lived there but he refused to bless the bones. Angelina listened to his protests and replied,

"A blessing might not be a bad idea, otherwise Elida could introduce ancient demons into the pantheon."

The priest changed his mind and gave the blessing.

The tower was home to the founders of Borgo and it suddenly occurred to Angelina that it was a waste of a tower to make it a home for an old priest who could easily move into the Borgo castle. That way his room could be a worthy eternal resting place for Elida.

The priest agreed to this too.

We explored the tower thoroughly. It had three floors and a raised platform so Elida would be the lady of her fortified tower, surrounded by heraldry and music because Angelina had granted her a Spanish music box that played ballads for dead princesses on a clockwork mechanism.

We picked up Elida, I took her under the arms and Angelina her feet and put her in her noble box but she scratched me with one of the bones of her left hand, where she had worn the ring. It was painful but I kept hold of her. I saw a speck of blood on her clothes and was suddenly terrified of gangrene. I remembered my esteemed professor Cristofredo Jacob. I wouldn't be brave enough to amputate my own finger.

"Don't worry, Chela, she's been around for several centuries, gangrene is a ptomaine that occurs in rotting organisms," Angelina tried to reassure me.

I wasn't convinced and had Vittorio take me in his car to find a surgeon. The doctor thought it was best to cut right down to the bone. As he worked, he used a machine to suck away the blood and I was given a glimpse of my phalanx, which was as delicate as Elida's. With my arm bound and slung to my chest, I went back to the top of the tower. Angelina said that the surgeon was an idiot and had cut too far. She was laying out the lady's objects and I decided to return her ring. That was when I saw that the speck of blood was just where her heart would have been, so, like a reliquary, she would keep something of mine while I would get nothing from her.

The ballads ended when the chest was closed. Now we needed to carry it to the highest part of the tower. Beforehand, we'd toast the event, the discovery and reunion with our ancestor, with Jeromian liqueur from the Caserta reliquary, wearing Spanish hoods and cloaks.

Lifting the chest was an enormous effort for my great-aunt because she was so small and for me due to my recent surgery, so much so we worried that our strength would give out and we'd drop and break our precious cargo.

After drinking the elixir—I'm afraid we overdid it—we saw the cypresses lining the path, eight in all, sprout arms and legs. Having attained the ability to sing psalms, they came to help us lift the deceased to her resting place: oh yes . . . they were the Capuchin monks who had lived in the tower in the eighteenth century, singing in praise of Our Lady. I shivered in an inner twilight more terrible than the deepest night and all its denizens while the eight of them marched steadily on with the chest and its beloved, terrifying contents.

And so traveled Elida de Zancle-Ucelli de Caserta, bejeweled in the Greek and Etruscan manner in a Spanish outfit for good measure. Unfortunately, at one point I told myself, "These are the effects of Saint Jerome's gremlins from the altarpiece," and my back crunched under the massive weight. I felt a terrible pain from dislocated, perhaps cracked vertebrae and to protect myself I returned to the dream, observing our eight attendants, the two in front looking at the floor and the six following behind, ramrod straight.

To whom was I offering this delirium? Whom did I have to curse or thank? What god or demon had blessed me? What was the nature of my spiritual state that I could carry such an enormous burden?

We walked up the spiral staircase, treading on green tiles decorated with tiny rhombuses up to the tower, right to the top, and then I was in the fields, the bridge, the chapel cellar, in a painful haze, wondering who was transporting whom, not daring to analyze a hallucination that sprang from my blue blood, an antiquity swallowed up in the air and the mist.

An incestuous entourage from out of a painting by Bosch during the reign of Philip II, or the proud Philippe Pot, whom hooded figures carry through the rotunda in the Louvre over rhombus tiles.

I remembered my friends from Paris on the night of the owl baptism, in the rain regurgitated by the Gargoyles of Notre-Dame, and relived the wonders of the country of the Carnutes.

After its enchanted journey, the relic was placed in its niche.

Today, I think it would be better to die rather than relive those experiences, and wonder whether we aren't just puppets in thrall to the underground societies who pull on our strings.

Returning Again and Again

I got back to the estate one day in October 1955, tired, with a half-amputated finger and an incipient hunchback after my enormous efforts.

I returned to my bastion, to my island in the grass, my Buenos Aires plains, and no one came out to meet me like Odysseus in Ithaca. There was just the strange air of neglected rooms, mold, the silence, and the damp because everything of mine had been locked away. Ariel had followed my orders.

I went up to the attic with Bertha, looked out the little window, and saw that the cabin in the garden was occupied. Then I heard the faint sound of a bell in the retirement home and the irascible part of me raged inwardly at the overthrown regime.

I kept watch and saw a man ride up, dismount, and tie his

horse to a post before going inside the cabin. I thought I remembered something from the time of Bertoldo and Juan Sebastián, someone who had aged rapidly, so that his face had grown corpse-like and his hair had turned prematurely gray.

With Bertha in my pocket, I went down, circumventing the chapel, and headed for land that had previously been the chapel graveyard and now was used to bury the former residents of the retirement home. I found Narciso tending to some flower beds.

"Miss, these are the graves of the old folks . . . when God calls them, they're buried here."

"In the chapel too?"

"No, miss, no one's been buried there."

I scratched at some moss on the stone of an old man rotting on my land. It was as though I were trying to scratch away the moss, stone, and hole all together.

"I need you to take me to La Plata, I want to talk to the administrator."

"You're not going to have them removed, miss . . . ? Poor things . . . they're flesh and blood like the rest of us."

Narciso wiped his tears on his cap and told me that the burials were overseen by the deposed mayor.

"Start digging them up right now."

He said he wouldn't, the poor creatures were resting in holy sanctity.

"Resting in holy shit . . ." I barked back.

Ariel came scurrying over in his customary way.

"My God, Chela . . ."

"Who's living in my cabin?" I spat.

"Go see for yourself."

I went up to the attic and slept for the rest of the day. Later I'd go see the de facto mayor and have him send me a clean-up crew. Ariel sent a girl in case I needed a maid. I was amused by her name, Dulce—Sweet.

Sometime later, Dulce told me that a gentleman was waiting for me in the garden. I spied in my customary fashion and saw the man with the gray hair and corpse face dressed as a peasant, beating his boot with this riding crop. I recognized the gesture and even heard the words "Helloooo, nutjobs."

Arnaldo . . .

I showed him into the main hall, which had witnessed so much childish and not so childish mischief, and the hijinks between my mother and Mr. Roux. Arnaldo stood waiting, looking hopeless.

"What do you want? Or were you just hoping to get an eyeful?"

"Chela, I want to save my wife, she's pregnant, and myself . . ."

"Save yourself? How?"

"I'm hiding in the cabin because I've been declared a traitor to the nation."

"Leave right now, or I'll go to the police."

He left with his wife in Narciso's car.

I put Bertha in her new terrarium and went down with a lamp full of kerosene to set fire to the cabin. I knew that Ariel was petitioning the authorities in La Plata to save the retirement home and the graveyard. Everyone was against me.

I got a letter from Messina whose black sash prefaced my grief. My second cousin, Diana Cerveteri de Caserta, was informing me of the passing of Angelina, and that same night, as though I hadn't suffered enough, I was woken by a croaking, a faint sound like something breaking down, coming from the terrarium. Bertha was lying on her back, a little piece of lettuce in her mouth. I cried. *Bertha, why have you abandoned me?*

The clean-up crew was authorized and by the middle of November the carts were entering the graveyard. I enjoyed the performance from my window.

The disinterred old folk were being taken away, covered in hessian. The scarecrows filled up three carts, their legs and arms sticking out from under the hessian, their wrench-shaped hands grasping at the estate air.

What I saw next must have been the effect of the pills, in which I increasingly indulged, uncorking the blue bottle and swallowing four at a time, without water. One of the dead, for whom there wasn't room in the cart, was carried away by eight hooded figures. The group was shrouded in a lilac halo and across the lawn and fields bloomed flowers with rhombus-shaped petals.

The resemblance to another ceremony was impossible to ignore. My daydream was interrupted by the disgusting smell. I felt a need to disinfect and purify.

I knew how to make improvised incendiary bombs and threw one with excellent aim onto the roof of the retirement home I had been forbidden from evicting. A crown of flame snaked upward, opening into a wonderful fan whose writhing slats spread across the lot.

Oh yes, I climbed up to my attic to watch with relish, poking half my body out the window, and saw scarecrows in their underwear, half-dressed, naked, in urine-soaked nightshirts, living torches rolling around on my recovered fields, and felt a rare kind of filthy pleasure. Some officials from the de facto government came to bother me with a few questions but soon left me alone.

I hired another crew to chisel away the cement and the red patio of the old Angelina house reappeared with its hole of discovery. I'd got my ghosts back.

I sat down on the worn step. Some chubby rats were sniffing scorched, empty cans, occasionally stopping to clean their whiskers with aristocratic hands. Scrabbling, like me, through an underground universe.

The objects shook as though they were atop a lake of lilac-blue jelly, the customary color, when I saw a pile of rags begin to twitch and, although I wanted to flee, I couldn't move. The pile of rags slowly took on human form, divided karyokinetically like a cell into eight hooded silhouettes carrying a prone old man on their shoulders, and headed toward me. I smelled the sweet scent of macerated magnolias, and felt a bony touch as though my skeleton had broken free and were now on the outside. I wanted to run away but could only wriggle, soft and pathetic.

I wriggled up the spiral staircase into exile. Dulce came to tell me that an old man wanted to talk to me. I went down, and there he was, the charred old man, his head barely attached to his neck, shaking with the chatter of castanets or rhythm bones.

I felt the pee running down my legs, just like when my father called me into his study. Suddenly the old man fell apart into bones in a great clatter, like rolling dice or a flamenco dance. I ran back up to my refuge, I didn't have to wriggle anymore.

Dulce appeared with a tray of food and a drink.

"Did you speak to the old man, ma'am?"

"There was no one there."

The girl contradicted me. She went over to the porthole:

"Look, ma'am, there he goes."

She diligently went down and caught him up on the path. The old man turned around and waved to me with a wrench-shaped hand.

"Ma'am, he's a crazy old man who says you already know what he came to say."

I lived at the estate for a year, during which time Ariel made every effort to avoid me. I planned another trip. I would do heraldic research, visiting castles and exploring medieval attics. I'd live in a different century. My goal, as usual, was Paris.

This time, I moved into a small atelier from where I could hear the bells of the Sacré Coeur, a garret over a store that sold votive seals.

In my dirty pants and worn blouse, two braids draped over my hunchback, sneakers, and sailor's sack, I looked like a beggar.

I went to churches deep in the countryside, looking for iconography and crests; I was able to obtain a ladder to help me climb into towers, I stopped wherever the night caught up with me.

Once again, I was the filthy creature no one looked at twice. Some thought I was crazy, others that I was a tramp, and I begged for alms to see what it felt like to live off people's charity. After wandering for weeks, a need to bathe brought me back to the seal store. Sometimes I worried I would bump into Jules, but it never happened.

I fluctuated like dust in the atmosphere: from Paris to Finisterre, through Provence, Auvergne, Perigord, Poitou, Normandy, and Burgundy. In Amiens, I saw the old man from the estate and I fled as fast as I could, without having to wriggle. To console myself I reflected that all old men look alike but in a high relief in Lisieux I saw him covered in flames. I was atop a ladder studying a crest and the old man stretched out one of his deformed limbs and pushed. I fell from a considerable height, crushing the finger that had been operated on, and saw that the wound had begun to fester.

I reopened it with a small knife; it was throbbing, something was wriggling inside. Through a magnifying glass I saw the little things eat and defecate, eat and defecate, inside the wound, and the sight of little tubes with orifices at either end disgusted me. I shoved my hand into a bucket of salt and water and squeezed. The smell of feces filled the room.

At the hospital, they cut off my ring finger, pinkie, and middle finger so that the now useless index finger and thumb formed a kind of wrench shape. I remembered Cristofredo Jacob's hand. I couldn't get to sleep at the hospital and recited heraldic terms like a lullaby:

> *Or, argent, sinople, purpure and*
> *sable, gules, French blazon and Italian blazon,*
> *ermine lining, counter-ermine, vair and*
> *countervair,*
> *vair en pointe and in pale, tricked and hatching,*
> *compartment, escutcheon,*
> *mantling . . .*

I'd specialized in Heraldic Science for a reason. Half dead, I invoked exquisite coats of arms, but I still couldn't get to sleep and searched inside for other images.

Eagle, double-headed eagle,
hydra, mermaid, harpy,
phoenix, unicorn, sphynx,
centaur, lizard, dragon statant.

None of this was to any avail. During my recovery I sat in a rocking chair and read the newspapers from my country, the way Angelina had done, and learned that Argentine currency was becoming devalued. The agriculture and livestock industries fell to pieces. Then the newspapers ceased to arrive. In a French publication, I read the headline "What Have the Argentines Done with the Richest Country in the World?"

Weaker than an eighty-year-old, I left the hospital, tried to cross the street, and was hit by a scooter. I told the driver it was my fault, I had taken drugs and wasn't walking on the sidewalk. Lying in the middle of the road, I burst into tears like a four-year-old. My battles, earthquakes, disasters, and conflagrations . . . especially the conflagrations, paraded before my eyes as though on film. I felt like the baby in *Battleship Potemkin*, bouncing down the stairs in my stroller. And for the first, only, and last time, I cried out, "MAMA." I limped on and bought a newspaper. My body now a sack of pain, I went into a café for coffee.

I folded the newspaper, I'd read it later. I took two pills with the coffee. Miraculously, I heard the opening chords of "La Violetera" start to play, encouraging my long legs to begin a clumsy dance, which if anyone had seen would have made me a laughingstock. My legs were the only normal thing about me, my body was shapelessly hunched above them with its lump acquired in the great battle of Borgo.

And there was my hand.

Today, I am only a little taller than Juan Sebastián and my great-aunt, my beloved Angelina. I climbed up to my attic with the newspaper under my arm. I opened it and on one page I saw Luis's obituary. He'd died a week before, the same day of my accident; a long curriculum vitae underneath the photograph said, among other things, that he was mourned by his widow, two sons from his first marriage and two from his second, grandchildren, and other relatives. Had I really dedicated every moment of my long, sorry existence to this ordinary man?

And though I already knew in my heart that it was useless, I tried to draw on my knowledge of the occult, learned from my aunt in Messina, to summon him, but he did not come because he had never loved me. I felt a need to isolate myself even further and scoured antiques stores searching for an altarpiece like Angelina's. No luck.

I went back to my home country and since then Ariel has looked after me. In his compassion, he went to a cabinetmaker and commissioned an altarpiece for me, a reproduction of the one in Messina that depicts the translator of the Vulgate and provided refuge for my Castilian relative. Ariel placed me at the back without making a sound.

Inside the altarpiece I keep little bottles of lysergic acid because I am unable to obtain a drop of Saint Jerome's elixir. I have lovely pillboxes filled with powders and pills that, when they dissolve in me, burst into truly wonderful journeys, making me realize how little I have really traveled. Life has scratched, broken, and mutilated me like all the rest of the Casertas. But I can't complain because I held my own. I thought that nothing could upset, wound, or burn me, like Ariadne in the Prado, until I came across Luis's second wife in that La Plata clinic.

But perhaps it's all just down to my overwrought, soulless blood.

AURORA VENTURINI was born in 1921 in La Plata, Buenos Aires, Argentina. She was an adviser to the Institute of Child Psychology, where she befriended Eva Perón. In 1948, Jorge Luis Borges awarded her the Premio Iniciación for her book *El solitario*. Following the Revolución Libertadora, she lived in exile in Paris for twenty-five years. She wrote more than forty books. In 2007, she received the Página/12 New Novel Award for *Cousins*. She died in 2015, in Buenos Aires, at the age of ninety-two.

KIT MAUDE is a literary translator based in Buenos Aires. He has translated dozens of writers from Spain and Latin America for a wide variety of publishers, publications, and institutions and writes reviews and literary criticism for publications in Argentina, the United States, and the U.K.